Praise for
A Cuckold Odyssey

I CAN DO IT BETTER

"A terrific piece of erotica that is hot, sexy, and fun to read. The characters are well developed with depth and complexity. The emotions experienced by the men and women in the story are explored in a way that brings the characters, and the story itself, alive to the reader [....] The erotic scenes are very well done, steamy without being overdone. It's a definite spank bank book, if you're into cuckold/hotwife fiction [....] I highly recommend this for cuckold/hotwife fans."

—*Putaine Musings*

"Yes, a thousand times yes. I love it when a book goes all mental like that, from the point of view of a character (with a little insight from the writer), and we go deep down the rabbit hole inside someone's head[....] I dropped right into this book like a comfortable chaise lounge, never getting lost, and never needing to read the book one – and that is the hallmark of a writer who knows how to pick up on a story while keeping a newcomer perfectly informed, and also very nice work[....] Recommended strongly for those wishing to dive deep into the hows and whys of cuckolding."

—Sylvia Storm, *eRead Erotica Reviews*

COME HOME WITH US

"It goes above cuckolding, gets into what it is to love and have a relationship, and goes there. It is really, once you get into it, an amazing piece of work.... Do I recommend this? Yes. Strongly so."

—Sylvia Storm, *eRead Erotica Reviews*

"*Come Home With Us* tells the story of a VERY modern marriage. Fantasies are the spice of a couple's life, but what happens when Rob and Tina take their fantasies one step further? What if Rob truly becomes a cuckold? Hot sexual escapades are a big part of the fun here, but underneath the marital covers are secrets that could change everything. What happens when they come to light? Those were the questions I savored while reading this cuckolding page-turner."

—Alex Hathaway, author, *Education of a Cuckold*, *From Housewife to Cuckoldress*, and *My Husband's Adventures*

We Make Our Own Rules

We Make Our Own Rules

A Cuckold Odyssey

Rob Matthews

fannypress

Seattle, WA

fannypress

Fanny Press
PO Box 70515
Seattle, WA 98127

For more information go to: www.fannypress.com

Cover design by Sabrina Sun

ISBN: 978-1-60381-478-2 (Trade Paper)
ISBN: 978-1-60381-479-9 (eBook)

Printed in the United States of America

Also by the Author

Come Home With Us

I Can Do It Better

Chapter One

THE COUNSELOR STOOD UP and shook hands with each of us in turn as we walked in. With a welcoming smile, he said, 'You must be Tina and Rob.'

My idea of a counselor is a man who smokes a pipe and wears an old jacket with leather patches on the elbows. This one did at least have distinguished gray hair and a neatly trimmed beard, but he was casually dressed in black chinos and a polo shirt. I was disappointed he hadn't made more of an effort to look the part for us, but maybe even counselors have to move with the times.

'Do have a seat,' he said, pointing to the mismatched chairs. Tina looked at him expectantly, like she hoped for some brilliant insights immediately, but all he said to start with was, 'I thought we'd have blackcurrant tea; I hope that's all right.'

When each of us held a steaming cup, he settled into his easy chair with a notepad on his knee. At least he had that part of the look right. Fixing Tina with a penetrating gaze, he said, 'So you're in love with two men.'

Tina nodded. 'That's right. There's Rob, but there's also Adam.'

He turned to me. 'At least you're one of them.'

'That's a huge comfort,' I said drily.

He didn't react, but looked back at Tina. 'How does that make you feel?'

Frowning, she seemed to be concentrating on a crack in the ceiling. 'Confused,' she said. 'I didn't want it to happen,' she added, casting a guilty sideways glance at me.

'What do you think she means by that?' he asked me.

I knew exactly what she meant. 'This wasn't the plan,' I said, spreading my hands in a helpless gesture. 'We thought cuckoldry would be like a game we could play whenever we wanted, and the rest of the time, put back in its box and carry on as normal. We wanted some guy to appear on demand, give Tina mind-blowing sex, and go away again, without affecting anything else in our lives. And we had that for a while.' He didn't say anything, but nodded slightly, encouraging me to continue. 'Before Adam, there was Kieran. He came round on a Wednesday evening. And as soon as he'd fucked my wife with his huge cock and covered her, the bed, the walls, and the ceiling with his torrents of cum, he left. He didn't bother us at any other time. For me, it was perfect.'

'Yes, for *you*,' said Tina, with a quiet snort.

He inclined his head toward Tina again. 'But not for you?'

She wrinkled her nose. 'No, like Rob said, he had a huge cock. And he made me cum every time, but it wasn't enough. I wanted …' she trailed off, as if realizing that she sounded like a spoiled child who'd gotten everything she wanted on Christmas morning but still wasn't satisfied. 'Whenever he came round, I knew *exactly* what would happen. Nothing ever changed. It was like having a two-piece jigsaw puzzle. However well the pieces fit, you soon get bored of putting them together.'

'There are more pieces in the puzzle now?' he asked.

She smiled quietly to herself. 'I don't even know how many pieces there are in *this* puzzle. I only know that some of the pieces are dark.'

'What do you mean by that?'

She took time out to give him a teasing grin. 'Do counselors have the easiest job ever? All you do is sit there saying, "What do you mean?" and "How does that make you feel?" '

He looked back at her, unfazed. 'There's a little more to it than that. You don't have to stay if you're not finding it useful.'

She grinned again. 'Only joking. What do I mean by that? Well, the first time I saw Adam, I wasn't attracted to him. He was handsome enough, but I looked at his gray hair and just thought, *No. He's too old for me.*'

She was being deliberately provocative, but he calmly replied, 'He's only ten years older than you. When you were in your twenties, it wouldn't have been so strange to be with a man in his thirties.'

She nodded. 'I know. But I think most of us have definite ideas about the sort of people we find attractive. For me, that idea was fixed when I was young, so I like a guy with a full head of dark hair. Gray or bald doesn't normally work for me.' He looked down and scribbled something on his pad. She gave him a knowing look. 'Either you've written, "No daddy issues" or "A big hot mess of suppressed daddy issues." I know what you people are like.'

He smiled enigmatically. 'So what do you like about Adam?'

'He's not like Steve, the first guy I went with when I started cuckolding Rob. I've always said Steve had studied the blueprints of my body. He knew it perfectly the first time.'

The counselor leaned forward, steepling his fingers. 'This is interesting. I've asked you what you like about Adam, and so far, you've told me you were *not* attracted to him at first and he's *not* like your former lover. Are you more comfortable talking about what he's *not* than what he *is*?'

Tina giggled. 'You picked up on that, did you?'

'I told you there was more to this job. Are you embarrassed talking about him?'

'Maybe,' she admitted, rocking her head from side to side.

'It's harder to admit someone's studied the blueprints of your *soul*. That feels even more intimate.'

'What do you …?' He stopped himself and rephrased the question. 'Would you care to elaborate on that?'

'From the moment we met Adam, it was like he could read our minds. And when he fucked me for the first time, he knew exactly what would turn me on the most. He didn't excite my body so much as my mind.' She paused and shrugged slightly. 'But once my mind was turned on, my body soon followed.'

'He took you to places you'd never been before?'

'I'd been there before, but he took me by the right route.'

This time he couldn't stop himself. 'What do you mean by that?'

'Well, one time I thought it would be fun if Steve compared me with another woman.'

'An unfavorable comparison?'

'Exactly. I wanted him to say she was prettier and sexier than me.'

'Did you enjoy that?'

She shook her head. 'It didn't work for me.'

'Why do you think that was?'

'I didn't know the other woman. So it meant nothing.'

'When you say Adam took you to the same place, but by the right route ….'

The corner of Tina's mouth twitched. For a second, she almost smiled. 'He compared me to someone I know. Emma.'

'Tell me about Emma,' he said.

'She's a bitch,' said Tina. Then she laughed. 'Don't get me wrong; she's my friend and I love her. But she's still a bitch— through no fault of her own. She can't help being young and beautiful with insanely perky breasts. And I suppose it's not her fault some asshole was right on the point of fucking me ….' She paused and clenched her fist, reliving a memory that was still raw. I leaned forward and put my hand on her knee. 'I was lying on the bed in my best lingerie. Mark was standing over me, about to get his cock out. Then Emma phoned and he went running to her like a puppy.'

'That obviously hurt,' he said.

'It did,' she said, nodding. 'I offered myself to him and he chose someone else. That's a tough one to get over.'

'Doesn't Rob have to get over something like that every day?'

She put her hand on mine and gave it a squeeze. 'But that's part of being a cuckold. He loves it when I choose other men over him. Just like he loves being *compared* to other men.'

He turned to me. 'You like being insulted?'

Folding my arms, I spoke slowly, 'Yes and no. A guy I talk to on cuckoldchat.com likes being called a wimp and a fag by his wife and her bull. I don't want that. But Tina's right: unfavorable comparison *is* part of being a cuck.'

Tina nodded. 'Rob would be devastated if I told him, "I've been with another man, but—oh, babe—he wasn't as good as you. His cock was smaller and he came even more quickly, if you can believe such a thing." '

'What's the point in cucking your husband unless you get better sex from your stud?' I agreed. 'But I do wonder why *Tina* wants to be compared to others. It goes against the rules of cuckoldry. She's the hotwife—there to be adored.'

Turning back to her, he asked, 'You agree with that?'

'Sure,' she said, with a smile. 'Give me all the adoration you've got.'

'And yet you like being compared to Emma.'

She rubbed the back of her neck. 'Well … it turns me on.'

'But, Rob, you're not blind to Emma's charms. Couldn't you—?'

Tina interrupted him and answered for me, 'He could, but it wouldn't work. He loves me too much.'

'Do you think that's true?' he asked me, holding his hand up to Tina to stop her talking.

'Yes,' I replied. 'I'd spend all my time making sure she wasn't offended or hurt by what I said. And you can't insult someone effectively with that attitude.'

'So if I understand what you're both saying,' he said, turning back to Tina, 'you find it easier to explore the darker areas of your sexuality with someone other than Rob, because Rob loves you?'

She took a moment to consider this, then nodded. 'Yes, that's right. When Adam uses his fingernail to scratch the word "WHORE" into my ass, I feel like he means it. Rob would write, "WHORE but you're not really—you're the love of my life." And I'm not sure you can fit all that on my butt.'

He leaned back in his chair with the triumphant look of a prosecutor who's found the weak point in the defense. 'In that case, why would you fall in love with Adam? It goes against what you say you want.'

Tina sighed and threw up her hands. 'I suffer from a psychological condition called *being human*. We don't always get to decide who we fall in love with.'

'If you find yourself equally in love with both men, won't you find it equally hard to experiment?'

This was Tina's opportunity to say, '*Equally* in love? Impossible! No one could ever equal Rob, my king amongst men.' But she didn't. What she said was, 'That's one of the problems.'

'So wouldn't it make sense to back off from Adam? Focus on Rob for a while.'

I liked this idea and nodded approvingly, but she gave him one of her wicked looks. 'When Adam rips my underwear, fucks me from behind, and tells me he'd rather be with my friend, it feels so … *wrong*!'

I didn't think the word "wrong" had ever been spoken in such a positive way.

'Let's try an experiment,' he said. 'Rob, tell Tina in what ways Emma is better than her.'

My brain froze. 'I suppose,' I faltered, 'Emma's slimmer.'

'And that makes Emma sexier?' he prompted.

'Not for me,' I said. 'I prefer Tina's womanly body any day.'

He shook his head and looked disappointed. 'Is Emma prettier than Tina?'

Feeling uncomfortable, I rubbed my hands together. 'Emma's pretty, sure. She's got glossy black hair, dark brown eyes, and a cute little bump on the bridge of her nose.'

'You obviously find her attractive.'

'He does, doesn't he?' said Tina, looking at me sourly.

I added quickly, 'But Tina's very attractive too. She's got a great body and a beautiful face. She's gorgeous.'

Tina smiled and nodded as if I'd redeemed myself. He just said, 'I see what you mean. You're not very good at insulting her. Let me try.' He turned to Tina, and said with professional detachment, 'Tina, you're an old slut next to Emma.'

Tina tried to look outraged, but her pupils dilated and she opened her mouth slightly, running her tongue along her top lip.

'She's prettier, sexier, and younger than you. When Adam fucks you, he's *always* thinking about Emma. And Rob is too, but he might not have the balls to admit it.'

She didn't look at me for confirmation. Her attention was riveted on him. 'So if you fucked me now, right here on the floor, you'd be thinking about Emma.'

'Every second,' he said, looking her straight in the eye.

'Let's see,' she said. She stood up and unbuttoned her blouse to reveal a lacey pink see-through bra. 'You think Emma's tits are better than these?'

'Cuter and firmer,' he said.

'Oh, I think you'll find these are firm enough,' she said, walking toward him. 'Feel them.'

'It goes against a counselor's ethics,' he said.

'To hell with ethics,' she said, tossing the notepad on the floor and straddling his lap. 'And forget all this counselor shit. Just fuck me.' She grabbed Adam's wrists and placed his hands on her tits. He squeezed them. She responded by putting her hands on his shoulders, pulling his face toward her and kissing him. She opened her mouth and their tongues met.

This was still the most difficult thing for me to watch. It was coming up to two years since Tina had first cuckolded me. I'd seen the woman I loved take cocks in her mouth, between her tits, in her cunt, and up her ass. The body I revered had been covered with other men's cum and people had called her a whore and a slut. But all of those were sex. A kiss was love.

I was glad when Adam moved his head down to her tits. He kissed around her nipples, making them stand out even more prominently. He took the left one between his finger and thumb and squeezed it hard through the fabric. She breathed in sharply, but the expression on her face was more excitement than pain. He used his forefingers and thumbs to rip a vertical slit in the left cup of her bra. Her nipple popped out. He bent his head down and sucked it. She moaned with pleasure and then gasped. Experience had taught me that was the moment when he sank his teeth into my wife's nipple.

She pulled up his polo shirt and he lifted his arms so she could take it off. She ran her fingers through the hair on his chest. I hoped this was for my benefit. She liked teasing me about my hairless chest and telling me how much chest hair turned her on. Kissing her way from his throat to his right nipple, she took it into her mouth and sucked it. He winced slightly when Tina showed she could use her teeth too.

Slipping off his lap, she stood in front of him and lowered her trousers. Her panties were the same transparent pink as her bra. I hoped she'd take them off before Adam had the chance to destroy any more of the lingerie I'd paid for. She eased them down, slowly revealing her cunt. She'd asked me to shave her the day before Emma's wedding and was keeping that look for the time being. I thought she must have shaved earlier that day because she was perfectly smooth. She stepped out of the panties and massaged her clit with two fingers before letting them slide down into her cunt. 'I'm ready for you,' she said in a low voice. She took her fingers out of her cunt and put them in his mouth. 'That's what a real woman tastes like.'

He stood up and took off his trousers and shorts. He was fully erect. His cock wasn't much bigger than mine, but Tina had often enjoyed telling me it was *better*. It looked better, felt better inside her, and most importantly, it didn't shoot its load too soon.

My wife lay on the floor, naked apart from the bra, with her left nipple poking out through the tear in the lacey fabric. Her legs were spread and her shaven cunt was on display as she waited for another man to fuck her. She looked like she'd been carefully posed to appear as slutty as possible. Was that an accident? I thought it unlikely, knowing the calculating way in which Adam stage-managed scenes. He had a condom hidden behind the teapot—so much for his counselor's ethics. Putting it on his cock, he lay on top of her. She craned her neck up so she could kiss him again, took hold of his cock, and put it into her cunt. As he started to move inside her, she let her hands roam over his back. Gazing up into his eyes, she asked him, 'Does that feel good … thrusting your cock into my wet pussy?'

'Emma's pussy is better,' he said. 'Tighter, hotter.'

'You bastard,' she moaned, kissing him again.

He continued to thrust into her, maintaining a steady rhythm. He showed he'd *also* studied the blueprints to her body, placing a series of quick, light kisses on her neck, jawline, and forehead. At the same time, he twisted her left nipple hard between his finger and thumb. This combination of light and hard touches drove her crazy. But the psychological games they'd played had already taken her most of the way. A flush rising from her neck to her face, she threw her arms back behind her head. A growling moan started in her throat, and lifting her butt off the carpet, she came. He thrust a couple more times before his eyes closed and he came inside my wife.

She grinned and looked satisfied, so I was surprised when she turned to me. 'Do you want to fuck me now, Rob?' she asked. 'Adam's had the best, but you can have the rest.'

'I'm so turned on, it won't last long.'

She laughed. 'So, what's new? Come on, babe, show Adam what a lousy lover you are. But don't cum without telling me first.'

I took off my trousers and shorts. Adam went back to his chair and handed me another condom. I put it on and lay down with Tina. As I put my cock inside her, I felt that her cunt was larger than normal, as if it retained the shape of another man's cock. This realization was too much for me and I didn't even manage a single thrust. 'I'm going to cum,' I said.

'Already?' she said, contemptuously. 'All right, get out.' She pulled the bra away from her breasts and held it below her neck. 'Cum over my tits.'

I knelt beside her and jerked my cock. 'Apologize for giving me such a crap fuck,' she commanded. This was a new facet of our relationship. I suspected she'd learnt it from Emma, who often made her husband, Ben, apologize for his shortcomings as a man.

'I'm sorry for giving you a crap fuck,' I said. 'I know it didn't satisfy you.'

'What else do you know?'

'I've never truly satisfied a woman.'

'Who *can* give me the fuck I need?'

'Adam.'

'And why's that?'

'He's better than me.'

I came over her tits. I was surprised I lasted as long as I did. I've never produced much in the way of semen. She had a splash on her left breast and another in her cleavage. 'You've made a mess,' said Tina. 'Clean it up.'

I lowered my head and licked my cum off her tits. I still didn't like the taste, but I was getting used to it. It was something

Tina had gotten into more and more recently, so she normally told me to do it two or three times a week.

'There wasn't much,' she said, looking down at her freshly cleaned tits. 'I think you need some more. Adam, can you …?'

He took the condom off his cock and squeezed the contents over her tits and belly. 'You know what to do,' she told me.

I did, so I bowed my head again and licked another man's cum from my wife's body.

'How does it taste?' she asked me.

'So much better than mine,' I replied, although, in all honesty, there wasn't much difference.

After I'd got it all, she sat up and gave me an affectionate look. 'Are you okay, babe?' she asked. It was her way of signaling the game was over.

'I'm fine.'

I stood up and looked over at Adam, who was watching us with a sort of benevolent patience. It struck me that he'd worn that expression for most of the afternoon—while we were role playing the visit to the counselor and while I was licking her clean. It was the look of a man watching a Disney film with his kids: he knew how important it was to them, but it wasn't what he'd have chosen himself. I didn't understand this, as *he'd* been the one who'd suggested the role playing. I wondered what was in it for him. The only time he'd looked really engaged was when he was fucking her in front of me.

'Did you enjoy that?' I asked her.

'Seducing my counselor felt naughty,' she replied, looking at Adam.

'You were genuinely getting into the session,' he said.

She nodded. 'In a strange way, it was therapeutic. Even though it was a game, it felt good to open up. We should do that again some time.'

'If you like,' he said, in a noncommittal voice.

I opened the door so Boris, our shaggy black Labrador cross, could join us. He was used to the idea that there were areas of our life where he could never go, but he loved the moment when he could join us again. He ran up to Tina and Adam for a reassuring pat on the head and then lay down next to me.

'Shall we order in Chinese?' suggested Tina.

'Okay,' I said. 'Make sure we don't get too much.'

'We can have any leftovers tomorrow evening.'

'I'm not here tomorrow evening,' I reminded her. 'Training course.'

'Oh, that's right,' she said, and I was pleased that she looked genuinely sad. 'When are you back?'

'Wednesday.'

'Only three nights,' she said. 'I'll miss you, babe.'

'Boris will keep you company.' I looked over at Adam, hoping that he'd picked up on the real meaning of those words.

She took the ripped bra off and dropped it in the wastepaper basket. 'When do you think you'll be finished on Monday?'

'Late afternoon, probably. Why?'

'Go onto cuckoldchat.com at six. We can talk.'

I frowned. This seemed a strange suggestion. 'Or I could phone you.'

'Let's chat on the site,' she said, firmly. She picked her blouse off the floor and put it back on.

BORIS GREETED THE MAN from the Beijing Noodle House with both a warning bark and a welcoming wag of his tail. I took the bag of food into the kitchen and spooned the various dishes into three bowls. I remembered the days when there were only two bowls. But I told myself for the hundredth time that I couldn't complain. I'd chosen this lifestyle, and as we'd explained to the "counselor," it wasn't something we could put back in a box when we'd finished with it.

We sat together on the couch, with Tina in the middle. Once we were settled, Boris took a running jump and spread himself over all three of our laps. It meant we had to eat with our bowls resting on our chests. Tina had the television control. She aimed it over Boris's back and turned on our favorite Saturday night crime drama. On the screen, a man was trapped down a dark alley surrounded by knife-wielding drug dealers. Adam had learnt our catchphrase and halfheartedly joined in the shout of, 'I do not have high hopes for his future!'

But he and Tina had also started playing a game called Crime Drama Cliché. They waited for a line like, "Can you think of anyone who might have wanted to hurt him?" followed by, "No, everyone loved him." Or, "Where were you on the night he was murdered?" followed by, "Are you crazy? You think *I* had something to do with this?" When they heard one of these lines, the first to shout, "Cliché!" scored a point. If Adam reached five points first, he kissed Tina on the lips. If Tina got to five first, she kissed him on the lips. I couldn't see much difference between winning and losing, but Tina enjoyed it.

An hour later, Tina had kissed Adam once and he'd kissed her twice. When the program ended, Tina turned off the television. 'What do you want …?' she began. She looked round to find me yawning. Sessions with a counselor are always emotionally draining and I was tired. 'Let's go to bed,' she said.

WE DIDN'T HAVE A king-size bed, but we'd found a way of making it work so we all got some sleep. Adam lay on his back on the right hand side. Tina rested her head on his chest. I didn't like my wife sleeping like this, especially when Adam put a protective arm around her. I should have been the one protecting her. But it wasn't all bad for me. I lay on the left of the bed and curled myself around her, which meant I went to sleep spooning her butt. And if I reached my left hand around, I could generally find a breast to cup. My hand sometimes strayed during the night, and I woke up touching another man, which was a strange feeling, but a price worth paying. When Tina's first lover, Steve, had stayed the night, I'd slept on the couch, so this was a huge improvement.

Boris had taken to sleeping on the landing. He'd realized the bed was too small for four.

Chapter Two

~

G IVEN MY USUAL SLEEPING arrangements, my first thought
when I arrived in the hotel room late on Sunday evening
was that the bed was too big for one. I lay down and spent a
couple of minutes starfishing, just because I could. I went to
sleep lying on my back in the middle of the bed. When I woke
up on Monday morning, I was in my normal position, curled
into a question mark on the left-hand side, but with nothing
to spoon.

The first day of the training course threatened to run over,
and I thought I'd have to fake a coughing fit to get out of the
room. Fortunately, the tutor wrapped up at ten to six and I
made it back to my room in time.

I know hotel minibars are a notorious rip-off, but I poured
myself a beer. Resting the glass on the bedside table, I sat on
the bed with my laptop. Tina and I were coming up in the
world; each of us now had a laptop. I logged in to cuckoldchat.
com with my embarrassing user name. When we'd set up my
account, we'd wanted *cuckrob*, but the site's spell checker had
changed it to *cockrub*. Tina thought this equally appropriate,

so we stuck with it. Tina's user name was already in the list of people in the room.

> cockrub has joined the chat room.
> hotwife37: Hey, babe!
> cockrub: Hi, Tina. How's it going?
> hotwife37: You can be proud of me at last.
> cockrub: I've always been proud of you. Why now particularly?
> hotwife37: I was at work today and David called me into his office.
> cockrub: And you finally punched him out? I AM proud.
> hotwife37: Not quite. We're planning a move into Asia and David wants me to head up one of the teams that'll make it happen.
> cockrub: That's great! You go, girl!
> hotwife37: It'll be more work but there's also a sweet pay raise.
> cockrub: We should go out somewhere to celebrate.
> hotwife37: Definitely. Adam suggested Al Pescatore.

It was an innocent-looking comment, but it hit me like a punch in the stomach. I stared at the screen for a long moment, hoping some other meaning would emerge from her words. But there was no getting away from it. She had told Adam the news before she told me. This was a serious breach of the rules. I was her husband and should have been the *first* person she came to with any news, good or bad.

> hotwife37: The only downside is David expects me to have an in-depth knowledge of Indian culture, etiquette, and business practices.

She obviously hadn't realized the impact of her previous comment, so I carried on like nothing had happened.

> cockrub: There must be a website explaining all that.
> hotwife37: I might have to go out there some time. That'll be an experience.
> cockrub: How's your Hindi?
> hotwife37: I can manage a spirited Namaste! After that, I struggle.
> cockrub: I'll ask Ishaan to come round and give you some lessons.
> hotwife37: Is he sexy?
> cockrub: It's unethical for a teacher to seduce his student.
> hotwife37: What if it's the student doing the seducing?
> cockrub: lol.

I wasn't laughing out loud, because I was still smarting from being the second person to hear the news.

> hotwife37: How's the course?
> cockrub: Not great. The tutor's a jackass.
> hotwife37: Doesn't know what he's talking about?
> cockrub: He probably does. But it's pitched at the wrong level. There are guys in the room who've been teaching for twenty years.
> hotwife37: And he's giving you the remedial class?
> cockrub: Totally. He had the nerve to ask us what PPP stands for.
> hotwife37: He didn't!!!

I could imagine the sardonic look on Tina's face as she typed that. She supported me in my career and never complained about being the primary breadwinner. But she sometimes implied that anyone who spoke English could teach it. She never seemed to believe me when I told her it was a highly skilled profession with its own jargon.

> cockrub: It stands for Presentation, Practice, Production.
> hotwife37: Well, ain't that something?

I was glad my laptop didn't have a webcam so she couldn't see me shaking my head in despair.

> cockrub: We all learned that on day one of basic training. And this guy was standing at the front looking smug like he had esoteric wisdom to impart.
> hotwife37: lol.

I was fairly sure Tina wasn't laughing out loud, either. Everyone pretends to be easily amused when chatting online.

> hotwife37: How are the next two days looking?
> cockrub: Tomorrow's more of the same, then on Wednesday we've got some ex-army types taking us out into the woods for team-building exercises.
> hotwife37: Rucking through the jungle with a rifle and a backpack? You'll love it!
> cockrub: I'm dreading it.
> hotwife37: Think how macho you'll look.
> cockrub: But who'll be there to notice?

As I typed this, I found myself guiltily wondering how my French colleague, Danielle, would react to me dressed up as a military man.

> hotwife37: Send me a selfie.
> cockrub: Will do. What are you up to this evening?
> hotwife37: Taking Boris for a run in the park. He says

hi by the way.
cockrub: We have a talking dog? We're going to be rich.
hotwife37: lol.

I took a deep breath before I asked my next question. I hoped the words on the screen conveyed a breezy tone.

cockrub: So just you and Boris tonight?
hotwife37: Adam's here as well. He's right next to me.

This was another punch. I shouldn't have been surprised: I couldn't remember offhand the last evening when he *hadn't* been in our house. But I thought it was understood that Tina wouldn't see him without me. After she'd admitted that moving in with Steve was a mistake, we'd made an agreement that she wouldn't have sex with another man unless I was involved. I was to be an essential part of every cuckolding scenario. So maybe Adam had just popped round for a cup of coffee and would be leaving soon.

Adam has joined the chat room.
Adam: Hi, Rob.

It explained why Tina hadn't wanted to talk on the phone. She wanted a three-way chat. My mouth tightened in angry frustration. I was used to Adam sitting on our couch and sleeping in our bed, but I thought I could at least *talk* to my wife without him horning in. However, one has to be civil.

cockrub: Hello, Adam. Have you only just got there?
Adam: No, I arrived yesterday, shortly after you left.

He'd been there twenty-four hours. It must have been a super-sized grande coffee. And how did he know it was shortly after I'd left? I pictured Tina rushing to the phone and saying,

'He's gone at last. You can come round now!' I didn't like the image, because that was the action of a cheating wife, rather than a cuckoldress. I had one throw of the dice left.

cockrub: What did you guys get up to last night?

This was Tina's opportunity to write, *Don't worry, babe, nothing happened. I remember the deal we made and it's important to me.*

hotwife37: Quicker to say what we DIDN'T get up to!

I had my answer. It was another punch in the stomach, but it also caused my cock to strain against the front of my trousers. Putting my laptop on the bed, I ran across the room to close the drapes. I took off my work trousers, hung them over the back of the chair, and sat back on the bed. My cock emerged through the flap in my shorts. I put my right hand around it and pulled a couple of times. I thought I might as well live up to my onscreen name. As I was pleasuring myself, the rational part of my brain told me that she probably hadn't *deliberately* gone against our agreement. It was more likely she'd simply forgotten it. While she liked to accuse me of being an over-thinker, she was often an under-thinker. She was spontaneous and could be hot-headed. It was one of the things that had attracted me to her. But she should have remembered something that was such a key part of *our* cuckolding relationship.

Adam had been in *my* bed with *my* wife while I was starfishing in a hotel room. I was angry, hurt, and turned on. Life as a cuckold had taught me that it was perfectly possible to be all three at the same time.

cockrub: So what happened?
hotwife37: About that ....
cockrub: What?

hotwife37: Adam and I were talking. We thought it would be fun to make you EARN the details.
cockrub: What do you mean?
hotwife37: If you want to know what went on last night, you have to do the things we say.
cockrub: What sort of things?
hotwife37: Painful and humiliating things. We have loads of ideas.
cockrub: And what makes you think I'd like that?
Adam: How hard is your cock at the moment, Rob?

Damn Adam and his intuition. And damn my cock for reaching toward the ceiling.

cockrub: OK. What do I have to do?
hotwife37: Jerk your cock for us.
Adam: He's already doing that.

I was annoyed that he was making assumptions about me without any evidence. I was even more annoyed that he was right.

hotwife37: True. Slap your cock for us.

It occurred to me that I didn't have to do anything. They couldn't see me, so I could wait a few seconds and say I'd done it. But somehow Adam would know I'd cheated, so I gently slapped the head of my cock back and forth between my hands for a few seconds.

hotwife37: And don't bat it around like a kitten with a ball of wool. Hold it in one hand and hit it with the other.

How much had Tina learnt from Adam? If *she* knew

everything I was thinking and doing, it could mean big trouble for me going forward. I checked my laptop to make sure it didn't have a hidden webcam somewhere. It didn't, but I still slapped my cock properly. I laid it across my left hand and smacked it with my right. Six times, harder than necessary.

> cockrub: Done it.
> hotwife37: How's your cock?
> cockrub: Red and sore.
> hotwife37: As it should be.

It was also harder and straighter than it had been in a long time, but I didn't mention that.

> hotwife37: I reckon he's earned a few details. What do you think, Adam?
> Adam: I think so. When I came round last night, your wife was wearing a black see-through babydoll with nothing across her breasts except two thin straps that barely covered her nipples.
> cockrub: Sounds sexy.
> hotwife37: It looked sexy too. Shame I wasn't wearing it for you. It was for Adam's eyes only.
> cockrub: I'm sure I'll see it some time.
> hotwife37: No, you won't.
> cockrub: Why not?
> hotwife37: We're not sure you deserve to know yet. How hard is your cock?
> cockrub: Very hard.
> Adam: Do we like Rob's cock being hard, Tina?
> hotwife37: No. We like our cuck to have a tiny limp dick. Why don't you tell him what to do?
> Adam: Go into the bathroom, let the cold tap run for a while, and hold your cock under it until it's soft.

I put the laptop to one side again and stood up. I went into the en-suite, turned on the cold tap, and held my finger under it. After thirty seconds, I judged it was as cold as it could get, so I stood on tiptoes and had to stretch my cock to get all of it under the flow. As the water hit my cock, it wilted in my hand. It was the first time I'd done something like this. Usually, when I wanted to get rid of an erection, I thought about my least favorite politician. I felt silly holding my cock under the cold tap and asked myself, *Why am I doing this?* The answer came back quickly: *It turns Tina on and it turns you on, as well. Don't try to deny it.*

I went back to the bed, with my cock feeling icy against my balls.

> cockrub: Done it.
> hotwife37: How's your cock?
> cockrub: Like a cold damp rag.
> hotwife37: More the way a cuck's dick should be, isn't it, Adam?
> Adam: Yes. I think we should give him a few more details.
> hotwife37: OK. You tell him.
> Adam: I took a pair of scissors and cut the babydoll off her. Tina stood in front of me, naked.

I waited for another message to arrive. A minute passed.

> cockrub: And then …?
> hotwife37: You need to do something else to hear what happened next, babe.
> cockrub: That's all I get for giving myself genital frostbite? Knowing you were naked?!
> hotwife37: Take a moment to think about that, Rob. I'm your wife. You're supposed to be the only one who sees my body, but last night I stripped in front of

another man. I let him gaze at my boobs, my butt, my
pussy.

Adam: If Rob's getting complacent about me seeing
your body, perhaps HE shouldn't see you naked for the
next two weeks.

hotwife37: That sounds like an excellent idea!

That sounded like a terrible idea. I replied quickly.

cockrub: You're right—I'm sorry. Seeing you naked is
the best thing that can happen to anyone, and I'm so
glad you were naked in front of another man last night.
I could never be blasé about it. What do I have to do to
hear more?

hotwife37: Tell me how wonderful my breasts are.

This was something I could do with real enthusiasm.

cockrub: Tina, your 34c breasts are beautiful. The
first time I saw them, I was so turned on, I almost
came immediately. At the same time, my heart ached
because I couldn't believe so much beauty was in front
of me. They're the perfect size, the perfect shape and
topped with the most exquisite nipples I've ever seen.

hotwife37: That's interesting. What do you think of my
breasts, Adam?

Adam: Disappointing.

hotwife37: You wanted to know what happened next,
babe. Adam made me apologize for my breasts. I said,
'Sorry my tits are worse than Emma's, Adam.'

I hated my wife putting herself down. But at the same time,
I couldn't touch my cock for fear that the slightest pressure
would make me cum.

hotwife37: Do you want to know what happened next?
cockrub: Yes. What do I have to do now?

I'd gotten the hang of this game.

Adam: Rob, there'll be a bottle of champagne in the
minibar. Open it.
cockrub: It costs a fortune!
hotwife37: That's ok. We don't mind wasting Rob's
money, do we, Adam?

I'd thought I was going to have a relaxing time, lounging on
the bed, chatting to my wife. I got up for the third time, went
to the minibar, and took out a quart bottle of champagne. As I
peeled off the foil and twisted the cork, I tried not to think of
the price tag. I couldn't imagine my boss signing this off as a
legitimate business expense.

cockrub: It's open.
Adam: Pour it into a glass.

I had only one glass in the room and it was still half full of
beer. I drank down the beer and poured the champagne. As
I did, the words, "Beer before wine will make you feel fine!"
floated into my head. I didn't know what was going to happen
with the wine so I had no idea if it would make me feel fine or
not.

cockrub: Done
Adam: Put your cock into the champagne.
hotwife37: Oh yeah. Get those bubbles working on
your hole, babe.

She was talking about a particular feature of my cock. The
hole where I cum is different than most men's in that it's a deeper

red than the rest of my cock and unusually sensitive. Needless to say, Adam realized this the first time he saw my cock. And so, one evening, he encouraged Tina to lay me down on the bed and drag a pointed fingernail across the hole. The pain was so sharp that I nearly screamed. But Tina was breathing heavily and applying her nail to the sensitive spot with such sadistic enjoyment that my excitement soon overcame the pain. Now, alone in a hotel room, I could feel my heart beating as I prepared to feel that pain again. Standing by the bed, I held the glass in front of me and dipped my cock into it. As my cock touched the champagne, all the bubbles transformed themselves into needles and zeroed in on the hole. The initial sting soon gave way to a burning sensation as the tartaric acid started work on my delicate flesh. I left it in for a count of ten, took it out, and lay on the bed again.

> hotwife37: Tell us how it feels.
> cockrub: It hurts even more than your fingernail.
> hotwife37: Mmmm.

Normally, there's nothing I find more irritating than people in chat rooms who type *Mmmm* to show how turned on they are. Somehow, I didn't mind so much when Tina did it.

> hotwife37: I think he deserves to hear about the REALLY naughty thing we did last night.
> Adam: As you wish.
> GoddessE has joined the chat room.
> GoddessE: Hi Tina.
> hotwife37: Emma! How are you?
> GoddessE: Not too good actually.
> hotwife37: What's wrong, hon?
> GoddessE: Marrying a rich man isn't all it's cracked up to be.
> hotwife37: I wouldn't know.

Thanks, Tina. It's not my fault teachers don't get well paid.

> hotwife37: But surely Ben gives you whatever your
> heart desires.
> GoddessE: He has to justify every penny he spends to
> his dad.
> hotwife37: What is he, 9 years old?!
> GoddessE: It doesn't matter. If your dad's also your
> boss and landlord, he has a certain sway.
> hotwife37: Don't you have a joint account?
> GoddessE: No, John didn't think it was a good idea.

I didn't like John, Ben's father, but I had to agree with him on this one. Something told me twenty minutes of online shopping would be enough for Emma to burn through all the money in a joint account.

> hotwife37: What are you going to do?

Ladies, we're in the middle of something here! I was lying on a hotel bed with a raging hard-on. Much as I liked Emma, I didn't want to hear about her troubles at that moment.

> GoddessE: I'm thinking of getting a job.

Despite having my mind on other things, I sat up and paid attention. Emma had never worked in her life. She must have been desperate if she was considering this step.

> hotwife37: Great! what are you going to do?
> GoddessE: Not sure. Can I come over some time?
> Wednesday round 8? I'd like to discuss this with you
> guys.
> hotwife37: Should be fine. That ok with you, Rob?

It was a casual question, but it made me feel better. Tina acknowledged that I still had some say in who came over to the house. In the past, she'd often invited people round without asking me, so this felt like a step up.

> GoddessE: Oh hi, Rob. I didn't know u were there.
> cockrub: Hi Emma. Yes, Wednesday's ok. I should be back late afternoon.
> GoddessE: I'm not interrupting, am I?
> hotwife37: No. it's fine.

Err ... hello!

> hotwife37: Adam's here as well. I'm kicking back and chatting with my husbands.

With your *whats*?

If Tina's previous comments had been like punches, this was like being thrown to the ground and repeatedly kicked. I read the message several times and even rubbed the screen, hoping the "s" was an unfortunately shaped speck of dirt. But there was no denying it: she had used the word "husbands." I had no issue with Tina talking about studs or bulls, because they both merely implied a man who had sex a lot and was very good at it. And I didn't mind Tina calling another man her lover because, ironically, there's no implication of love in the word "lover." It's just the person you're having sex with. I was even okay with "boyfriend." Growing up, I'd seen enough of my sister's relationships to know that boyfriends could be here today and gone tomorrow. I didn't regard a boyfriend as anyone special. But a husband was something different. I couldn't imagine the single letter "s" had ever caused so much heartache. What did it mean? He was now on a par with me? She'd been with me seventeen years. She'd known him a couple of months and that was enough to give us equal footing in her life? This was a violation of the most fundamental rule of a cuckold relationship. The cuck must be able to trust that, whatever goes on in his wife's bed, *he* is still her husband, occupying a unique place in her heart.

> cockrub: I've got to go now.
> hotwife37: Why?
> Adam: I think I know.
> hotwife37: Oh, babe, you haven't cum, have you?

It was as good an excuse as any.

> cockrub: Sorry.
> GoddessE: That's always been your problem, hasn't it, Rob?

We had definitely shared too much with some people.

> cockrub: I have to clean up. Talk to you guys soon.
> hotwife37: OK. LU.

That was some comfort, at least.

> cockrub: LU2.
> cockrub has left the chat room.

I wondered if I *should* cum. There was still a background hum of horniness behind all the hurt and confusion. But I thought it would make me feel worse. I'd have the pain without the excitement to offset it. I stared at my laptop some more, hoping for an alternative explanation. And, gradually, one emerged. Looking at the keyboard, it struck me that Tina could have made a mistake. This realization gave me a burst of hope. The S key was right beside the D. It would have been possible for Tina's finger to slip to the left and press it by accident. I could have confirmed it easily enough by calling Tina and saying, 'Hey, do you realize what you did? You wrote "husbands"—I mean, in the plural?'

And she could have replied, 'No way. Did I? I would never write anything like that on purpose, babe. You're my husband. My one. My only. No one could ever come close to you.'

I would have felt better and gotten on with my evening. But I didn't call her because I couldn't face the possibility that she'd say something very different. She might have said, 'Yes, because that's how I feel: Adam is the same as you, now. In fact, I want to have a ceremony to formalize it so we need to find a very progressive priest.' And I couldn't have coped with that.

I drank the champagne. My mind was in such a whirl, I didn't worry about the aftertaste of beer and cock.

Chapter Three

~

I DIDN'T WANT TO stay there on my own, so I went downstairs. The room where we'd had the training was now laid out for a buffet. Teachers from different language schools were standing around, chatting. At the end of one table were some plastic cups filled with white wine. I picked one up and drank the contents straight down. I shuddered as it hit the back of my throat: it tasted like nail varnish mixed with diesel. But I wasn't there as a connoisseur. I wanted to tamp down the churning in my stomach.

I drank the second one more slowly. Looking around the room, I saw Ishaan, who taught Hindi and Urdu, chatting to a woman. I wondered if Tina would find him sexy. He could come round, give her a Hindi lesson, they could have sex and then he'd go. A clean, simple arrangement. He noticed me staring at him and turned. I looked away quickly. The tutor was walking around asking people, 'Did you follow what I was saying today? Anything you'd like me to go over again?' He looked surprised when people rolled their eyes at him.

To avoid talking to him, I went in the opposite direction. The first person I found was Danielle, the French teacher. I *did* want to talk to her, even though something told me it was a bad idea. She was a reminder that I hadn't always followed the rules myself. Another fundamental rule is that cuckoldry is *not* the same as an open marriage. Part of the thrill came from the inequality of the relationship. Tina could have sex with anyone she wanted, while I had to remain faithful. I'd broken this rule with Danielle by having sex with her while Tina was living with Steve. In another relationship, this might have been a reasonable *quid pro quo*. But not in a marriage like ours.

I was angry with Tina, and spending time with Danielle was a feeble gesture of defiance. Danielle detached herself from the group she was in and came over to me. 'Hey, Rob, what are you up to?' she asked, using the latest idiomatic expression she'd learned.

She smiled and I remembered why she'd tempted me to break the rules. She was a beautiful woman—tall and slim with small breasts. She had long black hair, Mediterranean olive skin, and deep brown eyes. She was wearing a simple dark-blue dress that came down to her knees and looked effortlessly stylish. Taking a sip of wine, she made a face. 'How can people drink something like this?' she asked. 'In France, you would go to the guillotine for making this.'

They take wine seriously in France, so I couldn't be sure she was joking.

'What did you think of the course today?' I asked her.

She shook her head. 'Maybe tomorrow he will tell us how to brush the teeth and dress ourselves.' If people trying to follow him in their second language thought he was pitching it too low, he definitely needed to rethink his approach. 'How's work going?' she asked.

'My students still think I'll be happy if they explain something using the same words in a different order. I asked one guy what a fireplace is. He solemnly said, "It is the place for the fire." '

'That's not wrong.'

'I know. That was the problem. He was right but not in the way I wanted him to be. What about you?'

'I love the faces of English speakers when I tell them all objects in French are masculine or feminine. They cry, "Why is the table feminine? The table is not a woman! It's stupid!" '

I laughed and took another drink, feeling more relaxed. The wine might have earned its vintners the death penalty in some countries, but it was doing its job. She gave me a sly smile. 'Did you know that vaginas are masculine in French?'

I didn't know if it was her intention, but these words had the effect of making me think about *her* vagina, which, I remembered, was not the slightest bit masculine. I shook myself out of it and replied, 'That's crazy.'

'No, it's French.'

'Same thing,' I said, with a grin.

She slapped my shoulder playfully and our eyes met. It was the closest we'd come to having a moment since we'd had sex. Intimacy hadn't changed things between us. She could have made trouble for me at work, but even on the day I'd woken up in her bed, she'd walked into the teachers' lounge with a casual, 'Hey, Rob, how you doing?' I'd been worried when Tina and Danielle had met at the last Christmas party, but Danielle explained how, in France, most people celebrate Christmas on the twenty-fourth of December rather than the twenty-fifth. And Tina had done her best to look like she cared.

But now we spent too long looking into each other's eyes. 'How is your wife?' she asked, with an edge to her voice.

'She's fine.' My voice dropped as I said it.

'You are back together again?'

'Yes, but … it's not a normal relationship.'

She nodded. 'What do people say these days? It's complicated?'

'Something like that.'

She laid a hand on my arm. 'Do you want to talk about it?'

I looked into her eyes again and a loud voice in my head

said, *Don't do it! Walk away! Now!* But my mouth said, 'Yes, I do.'

'I have seen the buffet,' she said, with a look of contempt. 'It does not interest me. Shall we go and have something to eat somewhere?'

'Where do you suggest?'

'There are no good restaurants in this quarter. Let's go up to your room and order something.' I wasn't sure room service would give us anything better than the buffet. 'To save your reputation, I'll stay here for another ten minutes, then I will join you. Room number?'

'Two twenty-five.'

'*À bientôt.*'

I went back to my room, telling myself I had no reason to feel guilty. In today's world, men and women can be friends. We'd eat something, talk of this and that, and go to bed. *Alone. In separate rooms.* But even so, I closed my laptop and put it away in its case. My screensaver was a picture of Tina. I didn't want her looking at me while I was with Danielle. It was the modern version of a man turning his wife's photo to the wall before his mistress arrived. So maybe I did feel guilty.

Fifteen minutes later, there was a knock at the door. Standing outside was Danielle, carrying a bottle of red wine. 'You cannot drink the wine from room service either,' she said, coming in, 'so I brought something good.'

'I've only got one glass,' I said. 'I'll rinse it out for you.'

I went into the bathroom and cleaned the glass carefully. I didn't want her asking the awkward question, 'Why does this glass taste of cock?' She was sitting on the bed when I came back into the room. I handed her the glass, while I was reduced to swigging from the bottle.

'To old friends,' she said, touching her glass against the bottle. She paused to sip the wine and nodded, indicating that she found it drinkable. I sat next to her. 'So, what about you and your wife?'

This sounded uncomfortably familiar. It was the sort of question Adam had asked two days before. I told myself that *this* counseling session would not end up with anyone having sex on the floor.

I took another mouthful of wine and wondered how much I should tell her. 'There's this other guy she's seeing ....'

Danielle nodded. 'You told me she was having an affair with a man at her work.'

'She did, but this is someone else.'

'She is popular with the boys,' she said, with a wry smile.

'Yes, she is. She's an attractive woman.' I took another drink and decided not to hold anything back. 'I'm a cuckold.'

She frowned. '*Un mari trompé*?'

I understood enough French to know that wasn't right. 'I am not a deceived husband.'

'But your wife—'

'No one *deceived* me. I knew she was going to do it. I encouraged her.'

She frowned. 'Why?'

That was a difficult question. I thought for a moment about how to approach it. 'Have you ever asked a guy to spank you?'

She raised her eyebrows and gave a broad Gallic shrug. 'Possibly,' she said and looked at me hopefully, like she was wondering what I'd do with that information.

'It hurt, right?'

'A little.'

'But it turned you on. And part of what excited you was that it was someone who cared about you who was hurting you.'

She looked uncertain but said, 'Okay,' as if she'd agree for the sake of argument.

'Well, it's the same with being a cuckold. It hurts me *and* it turns me on when my wife has sex with another man then tells me how much better he was than me. And a big part of the excitement is because I'm being hurt by the woman who loves me.'

Though still confused, she was clearly interested. 'So, why are you sad now if this is something you wanted?'

'Imagine you asked someone to spank you and he took a big rough stick and beat you with it. Would you like that?'

She shuddered. 'Definitively not.'

'*Definitely* not,' I corrected her. Whatever was happening in my life, I was still an English teacher. 'It's the same with me. I wanted Tina to hurt me by having sex with other men, but now she's taken it too far.'

I expected her to ask what exactly Tina had done, but instead, she used another idiom she'd learned. 'Don't get mad, get even.'

'What do you mean?' I asked, even though I knew exactly what she meant. I was trying to buy a few seconds of thinking time.

She looked at me with excited eyes. 'Where is your wife now?'

'At home with her lover.'

'So your wife is with another man. It would make you feel better to be with another woman.'

The voice in my head immediately said, *No! Get out! Sleep in the lobby if you have to. Just get the hell out of here!*

But my cock said, *Why ever not?*

My cock must have transmitted some look of encouragement to my face because, without saying another word, she unzipped her dress. The last time I'd been with her, I'd told myself I'd never see her body again. But she let the top of the dress fall away from her shoulders to reveal she was wearing no bra. And once more I saw those small breasts with the chestnut-brown nipples. Last time, my cock had felt guilty and needed a lot of coaxing to get hard. This time, it was straining toward Danielle and yelling at me, *What are we waiting for?*

I kissed her. She tasted so different from Tina and didn't move her lips in the same way. Part of me wanted to pull back, but I told myself I was going to take revenge. When Tina asked me what I did on Monday evening, I'd tell her I spent it in bed with one of my wives. *Let's see how she likes it.*

I put my left arm around Danielle's shoulder. My right hand started on her knee and crept under the hem of her dress. I felt a jolt as I touched the soft flesh of her inner thigh. She sighed contentedly as my hand moved farther up and she parted her legs. It felt so good to touch her again.

And so wrong. But not *wrong* as Tina had used it—in the sense of being kinky and taboo. More in the sense that stealing money from widows and orphans is wrong.

I took my hands off her and rested them in my lap. 'Danielle, you're beautiful and I really like you. But I can't.'

She looked surprised. 'You did before.'

'It was different then.'

'Different how?'

'As a wiser man than myself once said, "We were on a break!" '

'But she is with another man and ....' She frowned as she tried to remember another expression she'd heard. 'If there's sauce for the goose, then ...' she trailed off.

'What's sauce for the goose is sauce for the gander,' I told her. 'But that's not how it works in a cuckold relationship. The goose gets as much sauce as she can handle. The gander's lucky if he gets to sit in the corner and make his own sauce.'

'I don't understand,' she said.

I could sympathize. There were times when I didn't understand this life at all. I put my arms around her again, but this time, it was the hug of a friend.

She stood up and hitched her dress back up in a resigned way. 'Can I take the wine?' she asked. 'This is going to be a long night.'

'Sure,' I said.

She picked up the bottle and bent down to kiss me on both cheeks. She started toward the door, but stopped and turned. 'You know, I had sex with another man after you,' she said.

'Did you?'

'Yes. He was better than you. His cock was like a baseball bat and he fucked me all night.'

I appreciated what she was trying to do and it did sound sexy in her accent. But I shook my head. 'Sorry.'

'No harm in trying,' she said and went out.

I sat on the bed. I had a different set of confused emotions now. My cock was mad at me and screaming, *Seriously? You had a gorgeous, half-naked woman in your room! How many more times do you think that's going to happen in your life?* But the rest of me was proud. However much Tina had broken the rules, *I* had been virtuous. Strictly speaking, I shouldn't have had another woman in my hotel room. I shouldn't have kissed her and I shouldn't have looked at her breasts or put my hand on her thigh. But otherwise, I'd been as pure as the driven snow.

Chapter Four

~

THE TRAINING ON WEDNESDAY made me yearn for the two previous days. At least all we had to do on Monday and Tuesday was sit in a room and feign interest in stuff we already knew. On Wednesday, we were driven into the woods, where a former Special Forces sergeant split us into groups. He gave us twenty-pound backpacks—the training budget didn't run to rifles—and told us to make our way to a rendezvous point indicated by a cross on the map. Hiking through the forest was good fun, to start with. But our teacher's bodies soon tired. The map made less and less sense as we went farther into the woods. We were soon grumbling that it was a waste of time and asking how the hell pretending to be soldiers made us better teachers. I did a couple of hours in the gym each week, so I was in better shape than most of my colleagues. The only exercise some of them got was lifting a coffee cup to their lips. Even so, my clothes were soon drenched in sweat. The straps of my backpack dug into my shoulders and my leg muscles ached with each step. After three hours, we were hopelessly lost. The sergeant's assistant found us and escorted us to the rendezvous point with a condescending air.

We were driven back to the real world for lunch. After I'd eaten, I felt better, but I still found myself nodding off during the afternoon debrief. Before driving home, I had a strong coffee to make sure I didn't fall asleep at the wheel. I was tired when I parked outside our gate at six o'clock.

Instead of going in immediately, I spent a few minutes looking at the house through the car window. Tina and I had bought it when we were first married. Both sets of parents had given us money as wedding presents, and we knew how lucky we were to be moving into our own place immediately after the wedding. I remembered how exciting those first months were. Trips to the store were magical because we were a young couple, buying what *we* wanted. If we fancied donuts and chocolate chip ice cream for dinner, that's what we bought. We didn't have to ask Mommy, and it didn't matter how good we'd been. In the evenings, we cooked the food we had bought together and ate it in front of our favorite crime drama. When we'd finished eating, we sat back with a glass of wine, even on weekdays. We were in our space, where we made our own rules.

Usually, we went up to the bedroom to have sex, but sometimes we stayed in the den. It was *our* couch, and we could fuck on it if we wanted to. We kept a spare pack of condoms hidden discreetly under a cushion. Tina would take off her top so I could kiss and suck her tits. I pulled my trousers and shorts down to my ankles and slipped a condom over my cock. Sometimes, Tina had her back to me, so I could reach around and massage her tits. Other times, she faced me and I sucked her nipples. Either way, it wasn't long before she grabbed the base of my cock so she could guide the tip into her cunt. When it was in position, she let herself drop down and my whole cock was engulfed by her. When she moved up and down on my shaft, I wanted it to go on forever, but I always came too quickly. There was something so overpoweringly erotic about having this beautiful, sexy woman on top of me that I couldn't control myself. The muscles contracted and my seed pumped into the condom. That was where the problems began. Despite the hours I spent licking her to orgasm, she was never truly satisfied. We started fantasizing about men who could fuck her the way she wanted. That led to Steve, Kieran, and Adam.

What had our love nest become? A place where my wife had sex with other men. This was something I had actively encouraged, and watching Tina with someone else was still the biggest turn-on imaginable for me. But there were times when I wished we could take a break and step off this particular roller coaster. One evening of normal married life would be good. It would be nice to go in, hug Tina, and hear her say, 'Sit down and have a drink, babe. Dinner will be ready in five minutes.' Though she'd never said that in all the years I'd known her, a guy could dream.

But Adam would be there and he'd fuck my wife in front of me. I told myself I'd get into it once it started, but it wasn't what I wanted at that moment. I also remembered that Emma was coming round. Emma was beautiful, sexy, and funny. There was an illicit thrill when I saw her, not just because Tina was jealous of her. But I'd have been happy if she'd canceled. I wanted to soak my aching body in the bath, watch TV, and go to bed early.

Blunt claws scrabbled against the door as I put my key in the lock. As soon as I was inside, Boris put his paws on my chest and licked my face. He was a reassuring presence in my life. Tina's feelings might sometimes stray, but I'd always be my dog's favorite. If I walked in with the pope and Mick Jagger, Boris would still be more excited about seeing *me*.

Going into the den, I found Tina and Adam sitting on the couch. Boris followed me, lay at my feet, and rolled onto his back. I had no choice but to crouch down and tickle his belly. I looked up at Adam and Tina and couldn't help but notice the resemblance to the king and queen on their throne and the lowly subject kneeling at their feet.

'Welcome back, Rob,' said Adam.

Thanks for welcoming me into my own home.

'How was the rest of the course?' asked Tina.

'Still hellish, but in a different way. This was the day we all pretended to be in the Army.'

'Nice,' said Tina, vaguely, as if she wasn't listening. Looking at her watch, she said, 'We've a couple of hours before Emma comes round. We thought we'd have some fun.'

'Look, I'm tired, and—'

She interrupted me. 'Adam and I have been doing something we've never done before.'

Despite my exhaustion, I was intrigued. 'What's that?'

Tina gave me a cruel look as she said, 'We're not sure you've earned that information yet, babe.'

'I walked several miles with a backpack—'

'We enjoyed telling you what to do when we were chatting on Monday. And given that you spent the last two days cleaning sperm out of your keyboard, you obviously liked it too.'

I didn't argue with this version of events. I wasn't ready to admit what had really happened, so I said, 'Yes, it was hot.'

'So we've decided to carry on like that.'

It was hard to listen to her saying "we," meaning her and Adam. I was used to this word meaning her and me.

'If you want to know what Adam and I did the last two nights, you have to work for it.'

'How?'

She turned to Adam. 'What do you think, b …?' She stopped herself from calling him "babe" in time. But the fact she even considered it was like a knife twisting in my stomach.

Adam smiled. 'Let's start with something nice and easy. Clean the bath.'

Tina nodded. 'That's a good idea. Go and clean the bath, Rob. Get it right, and I'll tell you what happened.'

I sat there, looking at her. I didn't think I liked this new game we were playing. 'I've had a tough day,' I said in a whiny voice.

'I'm tired. Would you ask a Special Forces guy who'd just come back from ops to clean the bath?'

'If he were my cuckold, yes,' said Tina.

'How's your cock?' asked Adam.

I wished he would stop asking me that. And I *really* wished my cock would stop being rock hard every time he did.

'Go on, then!' she said, with a sharpness that did not come naturally to her. She was trying to talk to me the way Emma sometimes talked to Ben.

As I went up the stairs, I asked myself, *Why didn't I say no? Where's the Rob who faced down Steve?* But as I knelt down to get the cleaning fluid and cloth from the cabinet under the basin, I was aware of my cock pushing against the front of my trousers. As always, Adam had read me correctly. Here I was, the cuck forced to do housework so I could hear about my wife having sex with another man. It was humiliating, but it could have been worse. At least they hadn't put me in a frilly maid's outfit. My cock was throbbing uncomfortably, and I thought I'd have to open my fly and let it out. But I decided that would be too much: the cuckold doing the chores with his cock out. I hadn't sunk *that* low.

I scrubbed the lime scale off the bottom of the bath, cleaned the scummy rings of shampoo from round the rim, and polished the taps until they gleamed. After I'd finished, I called down the stairs, 'Okay, it's done.'

Tina came up and entered the bathroom, looking grim. She examined the bath carefully, rubbing her finger along different parts to check that they were clean. She only needed a pair of white gloves to complete the corporal-inspecting-the-barracks look. 'Good job,' she said. 'You can come downstairs and join us now.'

When she was sitting on the couch next to Adam again and I was standing before them, she said, 'There's one more thing we want you to do, babe. I promise it'll be worth it. You're going to hear something that will blow your mind.'

I'd already seen so much. I couldn't imagine what else they could do. Part of me was keen to find out. 'All right, what else do you want?'

'Well ....'

The doorbell rang. Boris went to the door with his tail wagging, which meant it was someone he liked. I followed him into the hall, and opening the door, found Emma outside. 'I'm early!' she said, brightly, as if that could only be a good thing. 'Hey, Boris!' Before I could say anything, she was in the hall, tickling Boris behind the ear. Bless Emma. It would never have occurred to her that anyone could have something more important to do than spend time with her. We went into the den. 'Hi, Tina! How—?' Emma stopped when she saw Adam. 'Oh, hello, I didn't know you were here,' she said, awkwardly. Embarrassment accentuated her well-heeled English accent.

There had been some tension between Emma and Adam ever since she'd tried to seduce him and he'd told her he preferred Tina. He pretended not to be aware of this and stood up to greet her. She proffered her cheek and he kissed it briefly. Going back to the couch, he sat more snugly against the arm so there was a space between him and Tina. When he patted the seat next to him, Emma sat down. Tina's mouth tightened as if she wasn't happy with this arrangement, but she didn't say anything. And the first thing Emma did was give Tina a big hug, which seemed to make Tina feel better.

Tina pulled an ashtray from under the couch and placed it on the floor in front of Emma. Neither Tina nor I smoked, so why was there an ashtray in our house? We normally gave Emma a saucer. Emma took a pack of Yves Saint Laurent cigarettes out of her bag.

There was clearly no room on the couch for me. I could have sat on the other chair but I squatted down on the floor again. Boris was happy with this arrangement, which meant more belly-stroking time.

'Tina,' asked Emma, 'do you ever get sick of being a hotwife?'

Tina took a moment to consider. 'It has its ups and downs, but I still love it. When I'm in bed with these two, it's like Christmas Day.'

I wasn't sure the church would approve of celebrating Christmas with a threesome.

'Adam's a great fuck,' continued Tina. He inclined his head to acknowledge the compliment. 'And no one licks my pussy like Rob.'

Emma rummaged in her bag for a lighter and lit her cigarette. 'Do you ever feel like a slave?'

Tina raised her eyebrows. 'Not at all. If anything, I feel like a slave driver with two men on hand to do my bidding.'

Adam chuckled, clearly amused by the idea of himself as a slave.

I rubbed my nose and asked Emma, 'You feel like a slave? To Ben?'

Emma looked at me. 'I know. He's my little puppy who dotes on me … well, as much as his dad lets him. But why did I spend my wedding day with another man's spunk on my chest? Why do I get fucked by my husband's best friend? I do things that turn Ben on, and in return, he buys me stuff.' She took a long drag on her cigarette. 'We have a word for that.'

Tina shook her head. 'It's not like that. Ben loves you. There's no doubt about that.'

Emma thought for a moment, then nodded and smiled tenderly. 'Yes, he does. It's just that I've always thought of myself as being independent.'

Really, Emma? Before your rich husband, there was a rich father. How exactly has your independence manifested itself?

'I don't know if I've got time for a job—'

'It *can* cut into your day,' said Tina.

As if unaware of the irony, Emma continued, 'But I'd feel better if I had my own money.'

'What are you thinking of doing?' I asked.

Emma exhaled deeply. 'That's just it. I don't know. I

thought I could become someone's personal assistant. A rich entrepreneur could take me with him on business trips to exotic places.'

'To be a PA these days, you need to be good with Word, Excel, PowerPoint, databases …' Adam said.

I wasn't so sure about this. I could imagine some businessman wanting a posh English girl in his entourage. Even if she didn't do anything, she might add class to his operation.

Emma made a face, as if all this sounded too much like *hard* work. 'Maybe not. What about makeup? I know about cosmetics, so I could give people makeovers.'

Tina nodded. 'Possible.'

'How do you think Ben would react if you took a job?' asked Adam.

Emma sighed. 'He wouldn't like it. I mentioned it to him once, and he said, "Don't worry, I'll always look after you." '

Tina gave one of her snorts. 'It's the man's job to go out and make money. The woman stays at home and cleans. Welcome to 1894, people.'

Emma ignored her and carried on, 'But I think I can pitch the idea in a way that will turn him on. I can say, "If you were a real man, not a little boy in your dad's pocket, your wife wouldn't have to work. My job is just another proof of your inadequacy." '

I wondered how Tina would react to this. As a feminist, she'd no doubt deplore this sort of gender politics. But the cuckoldress in her would like the idea.

Adam put his chin in his hand. 'What if the job itself turned Ben on? Imagine if a large number of men were looking at you, wanting you, having lustful thoughts.'

She frowned like she didn't know where this was going. 'I'm not sure I—'

'Why not become a model?' he said.

Emma's face lit up. 'That would be wonderful. Jetting off

to Paris, Milan, Los Angeles. Posing on a beach in the latest fashions. Hanging out with actors and rock stars.'

He nodded encouragingly. 'I'm sure you can do all that in the fullness of time, but *this* might be a good place to start.' He pulled a glossy magazine out of the briefcase at his feet. The title on the cover was *Society Women*. 'A friend of mine—Spencer, his name is—runs this. He's always looking for new models.'

'What is it?' asked Tina. 'Features on garden parties and charity balls? Lots of women in posh frocks?'

'Not exactly,' said Adam. He opened the magazine and turned it round to show us what was inside. We saw a photo of a beautiful woman in her twenties sitting in an armchair. She was naked except for a diamond necklace, a gold watch, and a fur stole around her shoulders. In spite of all the luxury, she looked bored.

'Can I have a look?' I asked. Adam handed me the magazine and I flipped through it. 'Wow,' I said, 'a dirty magazine. I didn't think these existed anymore. It's like holding a relic of some bygone age.' On the next page was a photo of the same woman sunning herself on a yacht and another of her standing at the door of a country house. The final shot showed her next to a red Porsche Carrera. In every photo, she was partially or completely nude and surrounded by the trappings of wealth. And she always had the same bored expression. All the scenes were carefully composed, well-lit, and expertly shot. I glanced at the articles on the pages between the photos. There was a review of a five-star hotel. Another article compared different brands of Champagne. The last one listed the advantages of hiring a private plane over using commercial airlines. I didn't think any of them were aimed at people like me, so I turned back to the photos. I'd seen more explicit material and there was no suggestion of cuckoldry in the pictures, so there wasn't any particular reason why they should appeal to me. But I did feel my excitement building as I looked at them and I wasn't sure why.

'What do you think?' asked Adam.

'Hard to tell,' I mumbled. 'I'll need to take it away and study it in more depth.'

'Give it back, Rob,' said Tina, rolling her eyes. I tried to hand the magazine back to Adam, but Emma intercepted it.

Adam kept his eyes on me. 'You're wondering why you're so turned on.'

'Well … yes,' I admitted. By now, I'd accepted that Adam knew what I was thinking, so I didn't ask what had given me away. He'd maybe noticed a change in my breathing or perhaps I'd shifted my sitting position slightly as I'd felt my cock growing.

'It's because they all look so fed up,' he said.

I held up my hands in surprise. 'I didn't know I had a fetish for bored women.'

'That's Spencer's genius. He's tapped into a potent fantasy. Each photo sends a clear message from the girl to the reader, "I may be rich, I may have everything, but I won't be happy until you fuck me." '

Emma bent down to stub out her cigarette and immediately lit another one. 'I can look bored,' she said. 'How's this?' She let the cigarette hang limply from her fingers and gazed at me as if I were the most tedious thing ever. Her pretty face was perfectly framed by her bobbed black hair. Her look of boredom made the groove in her upper lip even deeper. 'What do you think?' she asked, looking normal again.

'You're a natural,' said Adam.

'It's hard to tell with your clothes on,' I said. 'Maybe you could—'

'Okay, Rob,' Emma broke in, giving me a mischievous grin as she pretended to start unbuttoning her top.

'In your dreams, babe,' said Tina, putting her hand on top of Emma's.

Emma nodded decisively and turned to Adam. 'I'm definitely interested.'

I thought Emma was confused about what she wanted. She resented her father-in-law for putting the brakes on her spending and also felt uncomfortable with the idea that she was essentially being paid to turn Ben on. John wouldn't have any say over what she did with the money she got from the magazine, but she'd be paid to play into strangers' fantasies. Surely that was worse in some ways. But I didn't say anything. I liked the idea of Emma posing nude.

'Could you let your friend know?' she said.

'I already have,' replied Adam, with a smile. 'You can meet Spencer this Sunday at two o'clock.'

Emma's eyes widened. I think she was more nervous about the idea now it had a date and time. '*This* Sunday? Ben has to go and play golf with his dad.' She looked from Tina to me. 'Can you guys come with me?'

'*I'll* be there,' said Adam.

'I'd like as much support as possible.'

'We're not doing anything Sunday afternoon, are we?' Tina asked me.

'I don't think so,' I said, casually. I didn't add that I'd cancel anything for the chance of seeing Emma naked.

'We can drive you there,' said Tina to Emma.

It was good to be half of Tina's "we" again. 'That's fine,' I said.

'I need to get there earlier,' said Adam. 'I'm helping Spencer with another shoot in the morning. So I'll give you the directions.' He turned back to Emma. 'And if you and Ben are free on Sunday evening, why don't you come round here for dinner?' He seemed to realize this was overstepping the mark, even for him, because he added, 'If that's okay with you two, of course.'

Tina looked at me. I nodded and she said, 'Yes, that'll be nice.'

'I'll make my celebrated Beef Wellington,' said Adam.

'Celebrated by who?' I asked him.

'By whom,' he said. As an English teacher, I love it when people correct my grammar.

Chapter Five

~

AFTER EMMA HAD LEFT, I was ready to sleep. Sitting still had made my limbs ache even more. But part of me still wanted to hear what they had done on the last two nights that was so mind-blowing. 'So, what do you want me to …?' I began.

'Do you mind if we leave it for now, babe?' said Tina. 'Can we go upstairs and have a normal evening?'

By most people's standards, there was nothing *normal* about our evenings. But in some ways, I was relieved we could enjoy ourselves without my having to do any more chores. 'We could just *show* him what we did,' said Adam.

We went upstairs, took our clothes off, and got into bed together.

'Rob, why don't you suck Tina's tits?' Adam suggested. 'I'll focus on her pussy.'

If I'd been a regular husband, I might have been annoyed by another man instructing me on what to do with my wife. But for me, this was good. It was another definite change that had happened since Adam became Tina's stud or lover or … whatever he was. I was now involved in the action.

Occasionally, I missed sitting on the sidelines, watching Tina getting fucked. But generally, I loved being a part of it. And Tina adored having two men on her, doing everything they could to give her pleasure.

Adam lowered his head onto her cunt. He parted her lips with his thumbs and teased her by working the tip of his tongue around her clit without touching it. I took Tina's right nipple into my mouth and sucked it. At the same time, I squeezed her left tit. Tina put her hand on the back of my head and clamped me tightly to her breast. A groan of pleasure was building in her throat. I didn't know which of us was making her feel so good, but I hoped at least part of it was down to what I was doing. 'Oh, Adam,' she moaned, setting me straight, 'that's incredible, but I want more.'

This was something that hadn't changed. It was still the stud who put his cock in the hotwife's cunt. She lifted her left arm to pull him down onto her while he put a steadying hand on the bed beside her. He was preparing to get on top of her when I noticed something. 'You don't have a condom,' I said. 'I'll get you one.' I sat up and reached for the bedside table.

'No, Rob,' said Tina, firmly. 'Keep sucking my boob.'

'But you can't—' I protested.

'Yes, we can. Adam and I have discussed it. He's going to fuck me without a condom.'

'It's more intimate,' said Adam, looking straight at me. He knew I'd be happier if sex between them were a physical, animalistic act, because he understood that someone being intimate with my wife was the hardest thing for me to bear.

'This is a present for my darling Adam,' said Tina, taking her own dig at me. She knew I didn't like it when she used terms of affection with other men. 'Now put my nipple back in your mouth and stop worrying, Rob.'

I didn't do either. My mind immediately went off to a disturbing place. Another guy I'd been talking to on cuckoldchat.com had shared a fantasy about his wife getting pregnant by her stud. This cuck was excited by the idea of his wife's body as the growing, visible proof of her infidelity. And he liked the notion of raising another man's child and paying all the expenses—having a reminder of what she'd done permanently in their lives. I never found this fantasy erotic. All I could think was how rough it would be on the kid. Imagine how he'd feel if he discovered he only existed because of a cuckold's fantasy. 'We need to talk about this,' I said.

'No, we don't!' said Tina, with that sharpness in her voice again. 'Trust us.'

'What ... is he going to pull out?'

'Err ... yes, he is.'

It was a notoriously unreliable method of contraception, but it was better than nothing. My wife took hold of Adam's naked penis and guided it into her. I was still worried about what might happen, but I had to admit the sight was arousing. When I'd watched men penetrating Tina's cunt before, there had always been something between them. No man had felt her vaginal walls directly against his cock. But Adam was experiencing total closeness and intimacy with my wife. He was feeling the heat, the friction, the moistness of her cunt.

And he was doing something I'd never done. When Tina and I were first together, she'd told me she had no intention of going on the pill. She wasn't going to risk cystitis, migraines, and hair loss to save me the trouble of putting on a condom.

When he was inside her, he kissed her again, passionately on the lips. He moved his lips to her neck, then down to her breasts, where he gently sucked and bit her nipples as he began thrusting. Although Tina had said it was Adam's mind she'd fallen in love with, she'd let him use his body, as well. His thrusts started slow and only moved in and out by one or two inches. He knew when to increase the speed and the length of his thrusts. An expert at picking up on non-verbal clues, he could tell how close she was to cumming by the flush on her cheeks and the volume of her moans.

The quiet, almost reserved noises she was making told me that she *wasn't* close to orgasm. So I was surprised when she looked up at him with a knowing smirk. 'So, Adam, are you going to pull out and cum all over me?'

'Is that what you want?' he asked her. 'Do you want me to jerk my seed over your tits? Or would you like it on your face and in your hair?'

'Ah!' she said, closing her eyes and running her hand over her breasts. She obviously liked both of these suggestions but still shook her head. 'I want you to finish inside me. I want to feel your hot cum hitting the back of my pussy.'

'No!' I said, putting out my hand.

'Too late,' said Adam. He closed his eyes and gave a sigh of contentment as he came inside my wife.

'Oh, yes!' said Tina. 'You've flooded my pussy with your cum. Stay inside me. I want to feel close to you for a bit longer.'

After a minute, Adam pulled out and kneeled up between her legs. His cock was still fully erect with streaks of cum all over it. 'Let me get that for you,' said Tina. She sat up, gave me one of her wicked looks and lowered her face toward his cock. She ran her tongue from the base of his cock to the tip three times, licking up all his cum. As she swallowed, she closed her eyes and smiled appreciatively, as if she were tasting a fine brandy. Then she moved his cock out of the way to clean his balls.

Most men, I imagine, would have given their full attention to the sight of their wives licking semen off another man's genitals. And it *was* a profoundly erotic thing to watch, especially after what had just happened. But my thoughts distracted me. When Tina was satisfied she'd gotten every drop, she raised her head and looked at me. 'Did you enjoy that, Rob?'

'Have you any idea how irresponsible that was?' I asked, sternly. I knew the bulge of my hard cock, clearly visible through my pants, was detracting from my image as the rational, level-headed one of the group.

Tina grinned. 'You're worried about having a little Adam running around?' I put my hands up to my head and clutched two handfuls of hair. She realized how distressed I was and her smile faded: she'd gone too far. 'It's okay, babe,' she said, softly.

'How is it okay?' I demanded.

'A couple of weeks ago, Adam and I took a romantic trip to a clinic—way out of town, where no one could possibly know us. We had his and hers blood tests. You'll be pleased to know we're both fine.'

I hadn't considered that aspect of it, which *was* good news. 'But—' I began.

She sat up and reached over to the table on her side of the bed. She took something out of the drawer, which she held up to me. It was a blister pack of pills. Two weeks' worth had already been used. I felt an overwhelming relief, but I was also angry—those conflicting cuckold emotions again. And I couldn't deny I was massively turned on. My wife had allowed another man to do something I'd never done. In the words of some of the guys on cuckoldchat.com, he'd fucked her bareback.

'You always said you never wanted to go on the pill,' I reminded her.

She gave me a cruel look. 'I never wanted *you* to fuck me without a condom, Rob. But now I've found a cock that I want to feel inside me. And I've found some cum worthy of filling up my pussy. Speaking of which ….' She lay back on the bed and spread her legs. 'I think it's time you ate your first cream pie, babe.' Tina had also spent time on cuckoldchat.com and picked up the lingo. 'This is a present for my darling Rob,' she added, throwing me a bone.

She'd moved around to clean Adam's cock and reach into the drawer, so some of his cum had escaped onto her thighs. As I lowered my head toward her, she opened her lips. His semen oozed out of my wife's shaven cunt like melted chocolate from a lava cake. 'Save the sheet, babe!' said Tina.

The sheet was beyond saving, but I dipped my head quickly

and licked up a large globule of Adam's cum. After I'd caught the sperm that was trying to escape, I put my tongue as far inside her as I could and cleaned her out. That's when I started to enjoy it. The womanly scent of her cunt soon masked the taste of his semen. And I loved licking her with no hairs to get in the way. When she was clean, I made to get up, but Tina pushed my head back down. 'I haven't cum yet, babe.'

I licked up and down her inner lips. I did what Adam had done and teased her with my tongue, close to—but not on—her clit. With the tip of my tongue barely touching her clit, I used rapid fluttering movements until she arched her back and shuddered out an orgasm.

Adam stood up and put his clothes on. 'I want to get some air. I'll take Boris for a walk.' He'd realized Tina and I needed some time alone. And Boris wouldn't mind: he was a walk whore who went with anyone.

After the front door had closed, Tina looked at me. 'Are you okay, babe?' she asked.

I knelt on the bed opposite her. 'You should have told me before doing something like that.'

'I wanted to surprise you.'

I shook my head. 'There's a difference between surprising a guy and sending him into a blind panic about the rest of his life.'

She put her hand on my leg. 'You're not panicking anymore.'

'No.'

'Anything else bothering you?'

Her use of the letter "s"—as in husbands—had done a lot more than bother me: it had almost driven me to have sex with another woman. At the time, I'd read it as a calculated attack on my position in Tina's life. Now that I'd had time to think about it, I realized it might have been something thrown out without much thought. It could even have been a joke. These possibilities were comforting, and I didn't want them taken away. I couldn't talk to her about it in case she provided a clarification I couldn't handle. So I found something else to complain about. 'I wish you'd ask Emma to go outside if she wants to smoke.'

'We haven't made her do that in a while.'

'We need to start again.' I used a pointing finger to drive home the importance of something I didn't really care about.

'Adam says the dangers of passive smoking have been exaggerated.'

'Does he? And is the way it stinks up our house an exaggeration too?'

She shrugged. 'I don't mind it.'

'Well, I do!' I said, more forcefully than I'd intended.

She held up her hands in a pacifying gesture. 'Okay, we'll ask her to take it outside.'

'And where did that ashtray come from?'

'Adam brought it.'

'What's he doing, bringing ashtrays into *our* house?'

'He thought it would be useful for when Emma comes round.'

'But *we* should decide if we want ashtrays in *our* house. We don't go around putting ashtrays in other people's homes. Maybe he wants to turn the dining room into the smoking room. In fact, why don't we let him redo the whole house however he likes?'

My voice had risen an octave and I was shouting. She looked at me like I needed to be restrained. 'Talk to me, Rob,' she said in a soothing tone, trying to keep the patient calm until the ambulance arrived. 'Why are you getting so worked up? It's only an ashtray. What's this really about?'

I still didn't want to tell her the truth. So I went with something less incendiary. 'Tina, you had sex with Adam last night.'

In most marriages, the husband accusing the wife of having sex with another man would be not incendiary but explosive. But our marriage wasn't like most, and Tina frowned as if wondering what point I was making. 'Yes, and I had sex with him again tonight.'

'But we had an agreement. You wouldn't have sex with another guy unless I was part of it.'

'You *were* part of it. You read all about it when we were chatting online.'

'But—'

'We knew we were going to tell you. We planned it that way: we only did it for you.' She looked at me with puppy-dog eyes and asked, 'Don't you like your present?'

As she looked at me, she couldn't stop a grin from spreading across her face. *Dammit*, I wanted to stay mad at her, but I couldn't help myself and started laughing. She laughed too and we hugged. 'I don't want to cook tonight,' I said. 'I'll throw a couple of pizzas into the oven.'

'We can do better than that,' she said. 'Adam's doing his sweet and sour pork.'

The color rose to my cheeks again. 'Is he? Well, maybe I don't want his sweet and sour pork.'

'Last time he made it, you said it was delicious.'

'I'm not in that place today. I'm having pizza.'

She now had the expression of a mother waiting for a child to ride out a tantrum. 'Have whatever you want, Rob,' she said, quietly.

AN HOUR AND A half later, we were sitting in front of the TV in the den with our plates on our laps. I made yummy noises to show how much I was enjoying my pizza as I tried not to focus on how good the sweet and sour pork smelled.

Chapter Six

~

ON SUNDAY AFTERNOON, EMMA came round at one o'clock. Tina and I were finishing lunch, so Emma joined us at the table. Boris sat at her feet so she could stroke his ears. She still looked nervous, but also more resolved than ever to go through with the photo shoot. 'John came round to pick up Ben for golf this morning,' she said. 'Some of my clothes were back from the dry cleaner's. And do you know what John did? He had the nerve to go through my clothes, saying, "What do you need three black dresses for?" and "Most of these blouses are the same—why do you have so many?" He told Ben, "Savings can definitely be made here." Can you believe it? I desperately need my own money.'

We finished eating and cleared away the plates. Boris realized we were getting ready to go out and jumped around with excitement. I had the painful task of explaining to him that he wasn't coming.

Emma had a pink sports bag with her. 'I've brought a few outfits. I'm not sure if clothes are provided at this place.'

'I don't think you'll be wearing many clothes today, hon,' said Tina.

Emma looked nervous again so Tina gave her a hug. 'Could you put my bag in the car, Rob?' asked Emma.

Glad to be of service, ma'am.

We drove out of town. Tina had Adam's directions on her knee. It took forty-five minutes to get there. When we saw the place, all three of us said, 'Wow!' in unison. It was a beautiful, old, three-story house in white wood with a large, covered porch.

The man who answered the door was not my idea of a porn baron. I could picture him conducting a séance, though. Equally, I could imagine him taking part in an iron man event. I guessed he was in his fifties. He was tall, completely bald, with dark, bushy eyebrows, gray-blue eyes, and an aquiline nose. His powerful frame was clad in a black silk shirt and black trousers. He radiated intensity and a keen intellect.

'Welcome to *Society Women*,' he said, in a deep rumbling voice that reminded me of thunder rolling through a valley. 'I am Spencer. You must be Emma. Won't you introduce me to your friends?'

'Tina. And Rob.' She pointed to us in turn, although he'd probably have figured out which of us was which.

'Super,' he said. 'Won't you come in?'

He took us into a sitting room, where Adam was waiting. He came over to Tina and kissed her on the lips.

'Let's get to know each other,' said Spencer, indicating a circle of black leather armchairs in the middle of the room. We all sat down. 'I would offer you a drink, but we have a strict no-alcohol policy. There will be water available in the studio.' He turned to Emma. 'So, what interests you about being a *Society Women* model?'

She looked taken aback. No one had said there'd be an interview. 'I ... need money,' she faltered.

Adam and Spencer exchanged patronizing looks. I could see what they were thinking. *The poor girl's never done an interview*

*in her life. She doesn't know that one never admits to wanting a
job for the money—however true that might be.*

'Anything else,' probed Spencer, 'or just the paycheck?'

'Well,' said Emma, 'the pictures in the magazine are … nice.'

'And how will you feel, knowing a large number of men are
looking at you and … finding you attractive?'

'I like being looked at,' she said, simply.

'Super. And what do you think your husband will say?'

'Well …' Emma began and paused. She bit her lip. I guessed
she was unsure how much she should reveal about Ben.

'He's submissive to her most of the time, so he probably
won't *say* anything,' said Adam, 'and if he *thinks* anything,
we're hoping he'll just be turned on.'

Adam's words seemed to give Emma more confidence. 'He's
also a cuckold, so millions of other men ogling me should be
his ultimate wet dream.'

'I'm not sure it's *millions*,' said Spencer, a little sadly.

Adam spread his hands. 'We can dream. And maybe Emma
will be the one to push *Society Women* to the next level.'

'And what about you?' asked Spencer, turning to Tina. 'Are
you also looking to appear in *Society Women*?'

'No, she isn't!' I said quickly.

Tina gave me a censorious look, as if telling me she'd make
her own career decisions. But fortunately she told him, 'I'm
here for Emma.'

He looked disappointed, but nodded and turned back to
Emma. 'Let's talk scenarii.'

With my English teacher hat on, I judged "scenarii" to be one
of those plurals like "foci." It might have been strictly correct,
but it sounded pretentious—especially when discussing a
shoot for a porn mag.

'I'd like to start with a few shots of you on the deck of a yacht,'
he continued.

Emma's eyes widened as she asked him—half-joking, half-
hopeful—'Are you going to fly me to Saint-Tropez?'

'Would that it were,' replied Spencer. 'But let me show you the studio.' He led us up four flights of stairs. The top floor of the house had been knocked through into one huge hangar of a room. The walls, floor, and ceiling were all painted black. A series of separately lit enclaves around the room contained the sets familiar from the magazine. The "yacht" was an eight-foot-long fiberglass model of a deck and bow railing, cut off where the bridge should have been. Behind it was a large backdrop photograph of blue sky and clear sea. The door to the country house was just that—a door. It was surrounded by ivy-covered stonework and had steps leading up to it, but there was nothing behind it except wooden supports. The only real thing in the room was the red Porsche Carrera, standing in front of a photograph of green fields and hills that suggested life on the open road. 'You see,' said Spencer, 'we can take you around the world with a couple of steps.'

I had to ask, 'How did you get a car up to the top floor?'

'We reinforced the floor, hired a crane, and removed a section of the wall,' said Spencer, with a dismissive wave of his hand.

'Isn't that a lot of trouble to go to just for a magazine?'

He gave me an exasperated look, as if thinking I was surplus to requirements.

Adam answered for him. 'It's not *just* a magazine. It's part of the *Society Women* world—'

'And that world is my passion!' cried Spencer. He turned back to Emma. 'So we start on the yacht, move to the country house, and then have a few shots of you in front of the car. How does that sound?'

Emma nodded. 'Fine.'

Something struck me. 'Aren't those exactly the same shots as in the last magazine?' I asked.

Spencer gave me that look again. I had the feeling he and I were not destined to become great friends. 'Yes,' he sighed, with an expression that clearly said, *And your point is ...?*

'So every magazine is the same?'

'We have a formula our readers appreciate,' he said slowly and clearly, like he was trying to be patient with a slow child.

'Doesn't it get boring?'

'It's what. People. Want.'

Part of me knew I should shut up, but the perverse part of me wondered how far I could push it. 'The same thing every time? Don't they ever—?'

Spencer was on the point of losing it, so Adam cut in again. 'Rob, you love the James Bond films. When you watch a Bond film, you want the gadgets, the car chases, the explosions. You'd be disappointed if they weren't there. Am I right?'

'I suppose so,' I admitted.

'It's the same with the magazine. The readers complain if we try to change anything. They send angry emails saying, "I was looking forward to seeing Camilla in front of the Porsche so why wasn't she there?" or "Angelica would have looked so good on the deck of the yacht—why didn't you show us that?" When people open our magazine, they like to know exactly what they're getting.'

I shook my head resignedly. 'You know your business.'

'Yes, we do,' said Spencer, firmly, and pointedly turned his back on me. He told Emma, 'I want you in a diamond necklace and a gold watch, with something furry around your shoulders.'

'Is that *all* I'll be wearing?' asked Emma, shyly.

'Not initially,' he said. 'We'll do some shots of you in lingerie, to make sure you're comfortable with the environment. Any questions?'

'No, let's do it,' said Emma.

Spencer pointed to a door leading off from the studio. 'If you'd like to get ready in the dressing room, you'll find a selection of lingerie, all sizes and styles.'

Emma held up her bag. 'I've brought some of my own underwear.'

'It's better to use ours. The readers will expect it. You'll also find a shower, towels, and a hairdryer.'

'See you in a minute,' she said, and went off to the dressing room, closing the door behind her. Spencer turned to Adam. 'I like her. She has a certain naïveté, but at the same time, she knows *exactly* what effect she has on men. The combination is delicious. If you can find a couple more like that, I'll be delighted.'

It made Adam sound like a pimp who was procuring women for Spencer. Despite all the money that had clearly been spent on setting this studio up, the whole business suddenly looked cheap. I wanted to grab Tina and Emma and get them out of there. But that wasn't my call.

'How are preparations going for the show?' asked Adam.

'Very well,' said Spencer. 'We have a venue booked that's full of character. Still a question mark over the music, but that's not what people are there for.'

I wondered what show they were talking about, but that went out of my mind when Spencer turned to Tina and said, 'While we're waiting for Emma to come back, maybe *you'd* like to pose for a couple of shots.'

'No, she wouldn't!' I said, firmly.

Tina gave me another angry look.

'Don't worry,' continued Spencer, ostensibly to Tina but really, I suspect, to me. 'I'm not asking you to wear anything other than what you have on now. I thought you might like pretending to be on a yacht.'

'Yes, that sounds like fun,' she said, with a defiant look in my direction.

I remembered the last time someone had taken photos of Tina. We'd been blackmailed and she'd almost lost her job. I told myself I'd stop things by any means necessary if she started undressing. We went over to the yacht set. There were some steps hidden at the back and Tina climbed up onto the deck. Spencer went over to a large wooden cabinet at the side of the room and came back with a top-of-the-range Olympus camera. 'Sit down and enjoy the sun,' he said.

She looked odd, enjoying the sun in jeans and a thick sweater, but Spencer didn't suggest she take anything off. His camera clicked several times. 'You photograph well,' he said.

'Now,' said Adam, 'look bored. You have a fabulously rich husband—'

'I wish,' said Tina, looking at me sourly.

Again, Tina, it's not my fault if society doesn't value teachers!

'Just pretend,' said Adam. 'You're on a luxury yacht and it's a beautiful day. But you're asking yourself, "Is this all there is?" '

She tried a bored expression. To me, it looked more like she had flu, but Spencer was happy. 'That's good,' he said, his camera clicking away. 'Let's try you with a prop.' Adam went over and handed her a diamond bracelet. 'Don't put it on,' said Spencer. 'Hold it and look at it like it means nothing. You're about ready to toss it into the sea.'

Tina was trying out different poses and expressions when the door opened and Emma came back in. All heads—including mine, I'm sorry to say—turned to look at her. She was wearing a black bikini with a faux fox stole. It was the first time I'd seen her body. She was slim without being thin, and her skin had a healthy caramel glow. Her breasts were small and firm, and I had the feeling they'd stay exactly where they were after she took the bikini top off. Spencer and Adam gazed at her in awe, like they were seeing Venice for the first time.

'Marvelous!' said Spencer, with a sharp intake of breath.

'You look amazing, Emma,' said Adam, reverently.

A pissed off voice from the yacht cut in on their rhapsody. 'I guess you won't be needing me anymore.'

Spencer turned to Tina and spoke quickly. 'Thank you, that was super. If ever you want to pose for *Society Women*, we'd love to have you.'

'Of course you would,' she replied, with acid in her tone. She stood up and came over to me. I could tell she was even more annoyed with me now, but she had nowhere else to go.

'Let's get *you* onto the yacht now,' said Spencer. He helped Emma into position on the deck and handed her a necklace and a gold watch. He took a great many shots of her. Occasionally, he gave her an instruction like, 'Raise your head—that's super,' or, 'Lower your right leg just a fraction—that's super.' But generally, he let her do whatever she wanted. She soon relaxed and seemed to enjoy being the center of attention. Spencer turned his camera over and reviewed the photos he'd taken. 'These are fantastic,' he said. 'You might be the best model we've ever had.'

'Compared to the trolls you've had so far today,' muttered Tina, bitterly. I tried to put a reassuring arm around her shoulders, but she pushed me away.

'Do you think you might like to get an even suntan?' asked Spencer, smiling broadly at Emma.

'What do you mean?' asked Emma, innocently, although I suspected she knew exactly what he was getting at.

'Could we get a few shots of you minus the bikini top? Only if you feel comfortable, of course.'

'Why not?' said Emma, and put her hands behind her back to undo the clasp.

Standing completely still, I held my breath. I tried to make myself invisible by sheer force of will but didn't quite manage it. 'Wait a second!' said Tina, loudly. 'If Emma's going to take her top off, Rob has to leave.'

Adam looked at me and smirked. 'Have you always wanted to see Emma's breasts, Rob?'

'Never really thought about it,' I lied. 'Surely it's up to Emma to decide who—'

'No, it isn't!' said Tina. 'I'm your wife and *I* decide whose boobs you look at. Now wait outside.'

Feeling like a schoolboy sent out of class, I slunk away. The door of the studio shut behind me. It was a solid door with no windows. There wasn't even a keyhole I could peep through. I went down to the ground floor and waited in the room with the black leather armchairs. I hoped there'd at least be some copies of the magazine lying around, but there was nothing. I had to sit and imagine what was going on upstairs. After ten minutes of this, I spent some time looking out the window. The house was surrounded by pleasant countryside and I contemplated going for a walk, but I wasn't sure I could get back into the house. So I sat down and deleted the old texts on my phone. Somehow, I managed to kill two hours until the studio door opened and they came down the stairs.

Tina was in a better mood and seemed to have forgiven me. She sat in the seat next to mine. 'Sorry, babe. I didn't realize how long that would take. Are you ready to go?'

'Yes.' I stood up and saw Emma in the doorway. 'How was it?' I asked her.

'It was good,' she said, nodding. 'I enjoyed it.'

We went into the hallway, where Spencer and Adam were waiting. 'Thank you so much for coming,' said Spencer to Emma. 'You were wonderful.'

He kissed Emma and Tina on the cheek and shook my hand stiffly. 'I hope to see you again soon.' He didn't direct the comment my way. I guessed he wasn't too bothered about seeing *me* again. We headed for the door.

'Are you coming, Adam?' asked Tina.

'Later. I've a couple of things to discuss with Spencer. What time's Ben coming round?'

'Seven,' replied Emma.

'I'll make sure I'm there to welcome him.'

We walked back to the car. 'What did you think of Spencer?' I asked, when we were far enough away from the house.

'He looked after me,' said Emma.

'He was okay,' said Tina. 'You didn't like him, did you, babe?'

'A bit of a creep,' I said. 'I wish we'd known more about him before we came here. We don't even know if Spencer's his first or last name.'

'He's Adam's friend,' said Tina, as if that were sufficient credentials for anyone.

'And we know where he lives,' I said. 'That's some comfort if anything goes wrong.'

'What do you think's going to go wrong?' asked Tina.

'What if he never pays up?'

Emma reached into her pocket and pulled out a large wad of cash, which she fanned out in front of us. 'I'm not too worried about that,' she said.

Chapter Seven

~

WE ARRIVED HOME AT half past five. I wanted to check my emails, so I made Tina and Emma a pot of tea and left them in the den, where they chatted away. The ashtray came out from under the couch, and the promise to make Emma smoke outside was quietly forgotten.

Boris followed me as I went into the dining room with my laptop. My left arm was hanging limply by my side as I logged in and Boris pressed his cold nose against my hand before rolling onto his back. I ended up spending more time rubbing his belly than checking emails.

Adam arrived soon afterwards. He had two bulging shopping bags, filled with the ingredients for Beef Wellington, roasted potatoes, mushrooms, and a chicory salad. He also had a cardboard box full of bottles of wine. He took everything into the kitchen, and a moment later, came back into the den with two glasses and an open bottle. 'You need something stronger than tea after the day you've had,' he said to Tina and Emma. They didn't complain.

He went into the kitchen and started cooking. Ben rang the doorbell at seven o'clock. I hadn't seen Ben for a while. He looked well but tired. He was being groomed to take over his father's business, and by all accounts, John was pushing him hard. The eyes underneath Ben's permanently raised eyebrows looked more careworn, and there were a few streaks of gray in his sandy hair. I gave him a hug when he came in: we cuckolds had to stick together. He went over to Emma and she stood up to kiss him. She had changed into a simple white shirt, which might have been one of his. But Emma could have worn a hospital gown and made it look like a Versace evening dress. Adam came out of the kitchen and shook Ben's hand. 'How was golf?' asked Emma.

Ben groaned. 'I don't think our new clients had played before. It was a real struggle to let them win, but we managed it somehow.'

Emma laughed and kissed him again.

'How … was *your* day?' he asked her, tentatively.

Adam answered for her. 'You can be real proud of her. Her first time modeling and she came through like a pro. Spencer was delighted.'

I wasn't sure if Adam should be talking like this. I didn't know how much Emma had told Ben. But he obviously had been informed of her new career because he nodded and said, 'I can't wait to see the photos.'

'I can't wait for all the men in the world to see them,' said Emma, with a roguish grin. I didn't think the magazine's circulation was that wide, but her words had the effect she wanted. Ben moaned softly. 'Everyone will want me,' she continued. 'I'm going to be a busy girl.'

'That'll be so hot,' said Ben.

'Well,' said Adam, 'dinner will be ready soon, so if you'd like to come into the dining room ….' The genial host—in *my* house.

We went through and sat down. Good smells were wafting in from the kitchen, but the only thing Adam put on the table was the chicory salad. '*Amuse* your *bouches* with that,' he said, sitting down at the head of the table.

Emma took a mouthful. 'It's lovely.'

'It is,' agreed Ben. He turned to Adam and asked, 'How do you know this Spencer guy?'

Adam swallowed a piece of watercress and answered, 'I met him when I was in Paris one time. He's much influenced by the shows at places like the Crazy Horse. The French instinctively understand that a naked woman is a work of art. And their attitude toward sex generally is less furtive, less mired in guilt.'

What he said was borne out by my experience with Danielle, although I couldn't judge the whole population of France from one person. But it seemed that, for her, fucking me had been little more than a pleasant way of spending an evening with no after-effects. She certainly had a free and easy attitude to sex, which I sometimes wished I could share.

Ben stabbed a forkful of chicory. 'Do you have a stake in this magazine?'

'I have an interest in the *Society Women* empire,' replied Adam, vaguely.

'Empire?' queried Ben. I think the nascent businessman in him was intrigued.

'It's still in the planning stages,' said Adam.

Ben looked thoughtful for a moment. 'What exactly do you do, Adam?'

I was hazy on this point. Adam spent many hours in my house and in my wife, but I didn't know what he did at other times. He'd always answered our questions on the matter with the platitude, 'I have a number of irons in the fire.'

He took longer than necessary to chew and swallow his mouthful of salad. I guessed he was using the time to calculate how much he should say. 'My father started off in sales,' he began. 'It was said that he could sell your own mother to you for a million dollars and convince you it was the best deal you'd ever made. When he'd accumulated enough wealth, he became an investor. He knew immediately which businessmen would become millionaires and which would end up as road sweepers.'

Ben looked confused, as if he wasn't sure how this answered his question. 'And now you do the same thing?'

Adam smiled. 'Similar. Before my father died, he made sure I was financially secure for the rest of my life. So I have the luxury that I don't necessarily invest in enterprises that will be profitable. I invest in those that will be *interesting*.'

Now that Ben had got Adam to open up, there was something else I wanted to ask. 'And when you're not sleeping in our bed, where do you live?'

'I tend to get bored if I stay still for too long, so I have a place near here as well as bolt-holes in New York, London, Paris, and a couple of other cities.' He obviously wanted to get off the subject, because he stood up, opened a second bottle of wine, and filled Tina and Emma's glasses. They took a drink, and Adam immediately topped them up. 'Don't be shy!' he said, heartily. 'There are twelve bottles to get through.'

This was excessive for five of us. And for the second time that day, I felt uncomfortable. I had the impression that Adam was trying to get Tina and Emma drunk. I didn't know why, and I had no idea what I could do. There'd be a howl of protest if I cleared away the bottles and said, 'Let's stick to coffee from now on.' I made sure I took only a few sips of the wine myself. Something told me I'd better keep my wits about me.

'So, Emma,' asked Adam, with a twinkle in his eye that seemed to confirm my suspicions. 'How do you feel about Tina?'

Emma put her hand on Tina's arm. 'I love her!' The wine made this sound more emphatic than I think she intended. 'She was my matron of honor. She taught me how to be a cuckoldress and I'll always be grateful for that.'

Ben raised his glass to Tina. 'So will I.'

Tina blushed and looked down, but she was smiling in a gratified way.

'Do you ever feel in competition with her?' asked Adam.

Emma laughed lightly. 'No, there are plenty of studs to go round.'

Adam leaned forward and persisted. 'Never?'

Emma looked straight back at him. Although naïve in some ways, she was a strong-minded girl, not the type to be intimidated. 'There was this one occasion when I thought some bloke preferred Tina to me.'

'And how did that make you feel?' asked Adam, slipping back into counselor mode and pretending not to realize she was talking about him.

Emma had a smug expression. 'I was disappointed at first. But I called Mark as we were driving home and he was waiting for us when we arrived. After he'd spent an hour fucking me from behind, I was fine and able to carry on with my day.'

Ben moaned with excitement at this recollection, but Adam didn't react. He carried on, 'Did you know there was a time when some … bloke preferred you to Tina?'

Tina stiffened in her chair. 'Adam,' she said, warningly.

But he wasn't going to be put off. 'Mark was with Tina on the night of your wedding.'

Emma's mouth fell open. 'What?'

'I don't think Emma needs to know this,' said Tina through clenched teeth.

'That's not possible,' said Emma, shaking her head. 'Mark was with me.'

'He was in Rob and Tina's room,' continued Adam.

Tina murmured, 'Oh, fuck it,' reached for the bottle and filled her glass to the brim.

'Tina was lying on the bed in her underwear. You phoned him and he came running.'

Emma turned to Tina. 'You were going to fuck my stud? I thought that was just something you made up to get John off our backs.' Tina looked at Emma fearfully, like she wasn't sure of her reaction. At the moment, Emma was surprised, but would that surprise turn to anger? 'You slag,' said Emma. Tina might have been expecting Emma to hit her. She wasn't expecting Emma to lean forward and kiss her on the lips. Emma's eyes sparkled and she gave a husky groan. She was both amused and turned on. 'You were trying to take Mark away from me?'

As soon as Tina realized it wasn't going to turn nasty, she played along. 'Only for one night. I was going to send him back to you afterwards.' She paused and gave Emma her wicked look. 'If he wanted to go back, that is.'

'Of course he'd have wanted to come back,' said Emma.

Tina gave an exaggerated shrug. 'I don't know. When you've had the best ….'

'Bitch!' said Emma with a laugh.

Adam looked pleased, like everything was turning out the way he'd planned it.

'You know what this means?' said Emma, giving Tina a wicked grin of her own. 'I get to have a free go with your man.'

For a moment, I dared to hope she might mean me.

'I can fuck Adam. It's only fair.'

This made Adam look even more unbearably smug. 'You think you could satisfy him?' taunted Tina.

'Best fuck of his life!' responded Emma.

'Okay, ladies, let's discuss this rationally,' said Adam. He turned to Tina as if chairing a debate. 'Tina, what do you think you have that Emma doesn't?'

Tina thrust out her chest. 'You have to ask?'

Adam nodded. 'Yes, you do have bigger tits than she does.' He turned to Emma. 'How do you respond to that?'

'I say bigger does not equal better.'

'So you think your breasts are better than Tina's? Can you back that up?'

Emma's competitive spirit had been roused and the wine was making her reckless. She started unbuttoning her shirt.

'Hold on,' said Tina, raising her hand. I was generally in favor of stopping things before they went too far, but this was not the time. 'You should know already, Adam. You've seen mine hundreds of times and you saw hers this afternoon.'

'True, but I need to make a direct comparison.'

'Okay,' said Tina. She pulled off her sweater. She had a t-shirt on underneath, which she started to take off.

'Just a second,' said Adam. *Another interruption?* If the ladies wanted to get their tits out, I wished everyone else would shut up and let them get on with it. 'Tina, do you mind Ben seeing your breasts?'

'I'm okay with it if you are,' said Tina to Emma.

'Ben,' said Emma, in that sharp-edged voice she sometimes used with him, 'ask permission to see Goddess Tina's breasts.'

'Please, may I see your magnificent breasts, Goddess Tina?' said Ben, breathlessly.

'I didn't say they were magnificent,' responded Emma, crossly. 'They're not as good as mine.'

'We'll see,' said Tina. She took off her t-shirt. She was wearing a lime-green bra that supported her tits perfectly. The bra was opaque but she was obviously excited because her nipples were pushing through the material. I had to agree with Ben: her breasts were magnificent. She paused for a moment to let the anticipation build, then took off her bra.

'Stop ogling Goddess Tina, Ben,' said Emma. 'You are going to get such a spanking when we get home.'

Ben moaned quietly at this prospect, as if a good evening had just gotten better.

I must admit I enjoyed the way everyone in the room was looking at my wife's breasts. Ben stared at them wide-eyed and said, 'Incredible!'

'And the spanking's just become a caning,' said Emma, sternly. She turned to Tina and conceded, 'Not bad, but wait until you see mine.'

I was excited and proud of my wife for being so beautiful and sexy. But I was also aware that she'd made herself vulnerable. 'Er … Tina,' I asked, 'do you feel all right?'

She frowned like she wasn't sure what I meant. 'Yes, why?'

'To be … like that when everyone else is fully clothed.'

'You're right. We need to even it out. Rob, Ben, get undressed!'

'That wasn't what—'

'Good idea!' said Emma. 'Come on, boys!'

I don't think it would have occurred to Ben to disobey. He stood up and took off his jacket. I found myself unbuttoning my shirt. I stood up and undid my pants. The last time Tina had suggested I show my cock at a dinner party, I'd assertively said no. What had changed?

Soon Ben and I were both standing naked in the dining room. 'Get next to each other,' said Tina. Ben and I stood shoulder to shoulder. I was deeply embarrassed, and I'm sure Ben was too. So why were our cocks both fully erect?

'Two handsome chaps,' said Emma, charitably.

'They are,' admitted Tina, 'and their bodies are okay. Rob still goes to the gym regularly.'

'There's a gym in the building where Ben works,' said Emma. 'He could do with more tone in his upper body, but he's not too bad. This is the first time you've seen Ben's two-inch prick, Adam. What do you think?'

'It's what I expected,' said Adam, briefly. 'But—'

'I like Rob's prick,' said Emma. Despite the uncomfortable situation, I enjoyed the compliment and could feel myself blushing. 'It's three times the size of Ben's. If I didn't know better, I'd say I could have a good time with that.'

'What would happen if Emma tried to fuck you, Rob?' asked Tina.

'I'd cum in less than a minute,' I admitted.

Tina snorted. 'Less than a second, you mean.' She filled her glass and topped off Emma's.

'You asked me to make a direct comparison,' said Adam. 'I didn't realize *this* is what you had in mind.'

'It wasn't,' said Emma and started unbuttoning her shirt.

'Wait …' said Tina.

Stop interrupting! If Ben and I were allowed to get naked, the same rights should be given to Emma. Equal opportunities and all that.

'Remember, Rob's not allowed to see your tits.'

Emma nodded, looked at my cock, and said, 'Do you think Rob's enjoying this too much?'

'Definitely,' said Tina.

'Because Ben certainly is. There's something I do every now and then that stops him getting too excited. Have you got any toothpaste?'

'Of course,' said Tina. 'Rob, there's a fresh tube on the top shelf of the bathroom cupboard.'

I went upstairs, with Boris following me. I had spent enough time on cuckoldchat.com to have a good idea what the toothpaste was going to be used for. I found the tube where Tina had said. Before I went back down, I looked at myself in the bathroom mirror and asked my reflection, *What's happening? A couple of years ago, you wanted to watch your wife having sex with someone else. That's one thing, but this is another. Is this what you wanted? But here you are, obeying orders without question like a good little cuck.* My reflection didn't have any answers, so I went downstairs. When I arrived back at the dining room, I shut the door on Boris. He gave me a mournful *What have I done?* look, but there were some things I didn't want him to see at his age.

Tina still had her tits out, while Emma was in her shirt, with the top three buttons undone. Another bottle of wine was empty. Adam sat at the head of the table, looking far too pleased with the situation. Ben had gone back to his seat at the other end. He was still naked and his expression was a mixture of excitement and nervous anticipation: he knew what was coming next.

'Ben,' said Emma, severely, 'spread your legs and put your

hands behind your back. Let them all look at your poor excuse for a prick.'

He was clearly mortified, sitting there with everyone looking at him. But he was also extremely turned on. His cock was as big as it could ever be. Maybe Emma was right: he *was* enjoying it too much. 'Apologize to Goddess Tina and Master Adam for your tiny prick,' said Emma.

I was used to her calling Tina "Goddess," but "*Master*?" I suppose we were all doing exactly what he wanted. "Puppet Master Adam" would have been more accurate. Ben mumbled out his apology.

Emma looked at the tube of Crest in my hand and said, 'Rob, I want you to smear that all over Ben's cock and balls.'

Tina gave a low, guttural groan of desire. 'That's nasty,' she said to Emma. 'I love it.'

I went up to Ben and knelt in front of him. 'Sorry, buddy,' I mouthed to him, silently.

'It's okay,' he mouthed back.

Again, I wondered why I was doing this. I could have said, 'No, I am *not* going to smear toothpaste over another man's junk! It's a stupid idea.'

But I squeezed an inch of toothpaste onto my left index finger and took Ben's cock in my right hand. It was the first time I'd touched another man's cock since Tina had asked me to oil Steve up so he could fuck her in the ass. This was a very different experience. Steve's cock had been big, powerful, and dangerous, like a policeman's baton. Ben's was small and hard, like a peanut. I spread the toothpaste all over Ben's cock and balls. When I'd finished, they looked like they were made of frosting and could have been a decoration on a porn star's Christmas cake. I looked up to see how he was taking it, but his face didn't show anything. He was gazing at Emma as if mainly interested in her reaction. My first thought was that she'd trained him so well that he was like a Samurai warrior, not showing any emotion no matter how much pain he was in.

Emma guessed what I was thinking. 'Give it time, Rob. This is a *slow* torture.'

I put the tube down and sat next to Ben. 'You know, it's only fair …' said Adam.

'Yes!' said Tina, with an excited gleam in her eyes. 'Ben, put some on Rob, as well.'

And still I didn't say anything. I had lost the use of that simple word—*No!* I parted my legs and let Ben kneel between them. He lifted my cock to give him access to my balls. It was the first time I'd ever been touched by a man. Physically, it wasn't so different from being touched by a woman. Ben had not led a hard life, so his fingers were soft and delicate. Psychologically, it was confusing because my brain was having trouble reconciling the two facts that I was a straight man and that another guy was touching my cock.

I forced myself to focus on the physical sensations. When the toothpaste first touched the delicate skin of my ball sack, it was pleasantly cool. I started to think it was a myth that toothpaste stung. After all, our gums are sensitive and we put toothpaste on those every day.

'I'll tell you what you *should* do,' said Tina. 'Ben, rub some toothpaste into the hole in Rob's cock where he cums. With luck, we'll hear him scream.'

Tina was drunk and horny—a dangerous combination. But I was shocked at what she'd said. This woman loved me, so why did she want me to scream? Ben found the spot on my cock and covered it with toothpaste.

Ben and I sat next to each other while Tina, Emma, and Adam observed us. Ben was the first to react. He made a hissing sound as he breathed in sharply. A moment later, I understood why. In the space of a few seconds my balls went from tingling to warm to red hot. Meanwhile, the hole in my cock felt like ten precision-trained wasps were stinging it at the same time. Ben had more experience with this and seemed to be controlling the pain through deep breathing and focusing on Emma. It was the first time for me so my instinct was to cover the painful area with my hand. I did this too vigorously and ended up smacking myself in the balls, which Emma and Tina found hilarious. After this, I grabbed the seat of my chair with both hands and swore. 'Fuck! Oh, fuck!'

Emma held up her hand so Tina could give her a high five.

'This is good value,' said Tina. 'I must remember this.' She gave Emma a mock confrontational look. 'But we still have unfinished business.'

'Indeed we do,' said Emma. 'Are you ready to be jealous?'

She undid the fourth button of her shirt, but Tina held up a hand to stop her. *Will you just let the poor girl get her tits out!* 'You're forgetting, Rob's not allowed to see your boobs.'

Sitting there with toothpaste on my balls, I thought I deserved a special dispensation.

Adam said, 'Ben, why don't you find something to blindfold Rob with?'

Ben picked up his shirt. It was his turn to say, 'Sorry, buddy.' I didn't respond. He draped the shirt over my face and tied the sleeves together behind my head. Deprived of vision, my other senses were heightened. I smelled traces of expensive cologne on Ben's shirt and heard Emma undoing her buttons. I opened my eyes wide and tried unsuccessfully to develop X-ray vision.

'Tina, what do you think of Emma's tits?' asked Adam.

'They're so small and cute,' said Tina. 'Those little pink nipples are adorable. I'd love to kiss and suck them.' She seemed to have forgotten that she was supposed to be in competition with Emma. Tina had fantasized about other women before, but I'd always assumed she was only doing it to turn me on. This was the first time I'd heard her talking like this about a real woman.

'And Emma, what do you think of Tina's?'

Emma began tentatively, 'They're too big.'

'Not pert like yours?' prompted Adam.

'No, they're saggy.'

'Do you hate them?'

'Yes, I hate them. Fucking melons, she's got.'

'I hate them too. They're horrible. I much prefer yours.'

'Everyone prefers mine,' said Emma. 'That includes Rob. You've got shit tits, Tina. Even your husband hates them.'

That's when I lost it. Something in my brain snapped. I was sitting naked in my dining room with another man's shirt over my head and my balls covered in toothpaste. I was listening to people insult my wife's breasts. How had my life gotten to this point? What would my mother say if she could see me now? It made no sense that any of this was happening. I stood up, and ripping the shirt off my head, shouted, 'Enough!'

Ben looked at me in shock. He would never have dared do anything like this. Emma was too quick for me and had folded her arms across her chest before I could see her tits. Adam watched me calmly, as if curious about what I'd do next.

Tina gave me the look of death. 'Rob, what the hell are you doing?' she demanded, with a snarl. The fact that she was topless made her, if anything, more intimidating. She looked like an Amazon warrior about to reach for her sword.

I tried not to look at her as I said, 'I want everyone to leave now.' Naked and covered with toothpaste, I was finding it difficult to act the dominant male, but Emma put her shirt on, while still keeping her breasts covered. Ben followed what she did. As soon as they were both fully dressed, they headed for the door. Emma shook her head, like she couldn't believe some people. At the door, Ben stopped and turned. I think he was about to say, 'Good night and thank you for a lovely evening,' out of sheer habit, but he realized this wasn't the moment. He lowered his head and followed Emma out of the house.

Adam was looking at me with a quiet smile. 'Can you leave too, please, Adam?' I asked him.

'Of course,' he said. 'Officially, this is your house.'

His use of the word "officially" made me want to punch the smile off his face. But he left without another word and the front door closed behind him. I was alone with Tina. I'd have to do some smooth talking to put things right, but I couldn't concentrate with my balls stinging. 'Excuse me a moment,' I said. I ran upstairs to the bathroom and quickly washed off the toothpaste. By the time I'd finished, Tina's washcloth was a white, sticky mess. She'd be pissed about this but something told me it would be even worse if I left her alone for too long. I went into the bedroom and pulled on the first clothes that came to hand—a pair of jeans and an old black t-shirt. I went downstairs and into the dining room. Tina was sitting at the table with a glass of wine in her hand, gazing with tightly pursed lips at nothing in particular. She hadn't bothered to put her top back on. I sat next to her and poured myself a glass. She looked at me with anger and—yes —dislike.

'Tina, listen …' I said in a soft, low voice.

But my tone unleashed all the anger inside her. She screamed at me, 'Where do you get off ordering *my* friends out of *my* house?'

'I did it to protect you!' I shouted back.

'I don't need protecting.'

'Adam and Emma insulted you.'

She made an impassioned gesture, almost spilling her wine. 'To turn me on! Adam loves my tits. And I'm pretty sure Emma was jealous as hell. Ben will have to spend a lot of money before she has boobs like these.'

'You don't think it was all going too far?'

'All I know is I was so horny I could hardly breathe. My heart was pounding and my pussy was so wet, it was soaking through my panties and staining my jeans. I wanted Adam. I wanted you. I even wanted Emma. I wanted everything. And you stopped me!'

She looked at me through angry tears. I tried to calm her down and make my voice soothing again. 'Can't you see what's happening here?'

She folded her arms and gave me a sardonic look. 'So you're Mister Insight now. Okay, Rob, tell me what's happening.'

'Listen, Tina, you started falling in love with Adam when he turned Emma down to be with you.'

I could see from her eyes that she knew this to be true but she simply said, 'Well?'

'He waited until you were in love with him before he made his move on her.'

I was fairly sure she knew that was true as well, but she didn't say anything.

'I understand,' I continued, putting my hand on her shoulder. 'Tina, I enjoy watching you having sex with other men *because* you're the woman I love. Adam knows it will have a much more profound effect on you if you love him. It won't be just your stud fucking your hotwife rival: it'll be the man you love.'

'And he thinks that will turn me on?' she asked, in a more rational tone.

'Knowing Adam, he's intrigued to see *how* you'll react. I sometimes feel like we're rats in his lab.'

'I'm intrigued too,' she said.

'You *want* Adam to fuck Emma?' I asked.

She was silent for a moment, then looked at me with flashing eyes. 'Yes, I do! I want him to fuck her in front of me and tell me she's the best he's ever had. I want them both to insult me in the filthiest, most degrading way possible.'

I took my hand away from her. Even after everything that had happened, I was shocked to hear her talk like this. 'But why?'

Her face had a wild, possessed look as she declaimed, 'Because I want to try everything. I want to experiment. I want to go to different places—and if some of those places are dark, that's fine, because that's what I want too. I need to experience the darkness.'

Hearing my wife talk like this was frightening. 'But it's getting to be too much for me,' was all I could say.

There was no softening in her look. 'That's a pity, because I'm just getting started. I love you, Rob, but if you can't come with me to those dark places, I know someone who can.'

'But he betrayed you. He told Emma about you and Mark.' I was clutching at straws.

She shrugged. 'You take the good, you take the bad.'

'Well, I don't like where he's taking you—taking *us*.'

There was a metallic clang to her voice as she said, 'Too bad.'

I looked into her eyes. I realized I was hoping there'd be a different sort of tears in them. As terrible as it is to want to see your wife cry, I needed to know that she was conflicted. But the tears had dried. The manic look had faded. Nothing was left but a steely determination.

A large part of me was screaming, *Don't say it! Say anything, just don't say that!* But I couldn't stop myself. I looked at her and said, in the most measured voice I could manage, 'It's him or me.'

She didn't say anything. She looked at me with cold, unyielding eyes. I must have gazed at her for a full minute, but there was no change in her resolve. I couldn't stand it and ran out of the room. Grabbing my coat from the hook in the hall, I left the house. Adam was standing outside with that knowing look on his face. 'You made Tina choose between her two husbands,' he said, making the final "s" buzz for a second longer than necessary, 'and you didn't win.'

'Apparently not,' I said, tonelessly.

'*You* are Tina's husband, Rob. That's not going to change. Now come back inside and let's talk. The Beef Wellington will be ready by now.'

'I'm going,' I said.

For the first time since I'd known him, he looked unsure of himself. 'No, you can't do that, Rob. We need to sort this out.'

He stepped inside the house and held the door open for me. I grabbed the handle and pulled it shut. For a moment, I felt a rush of victory. And then it hit me that I was outside, alone.

Chapter Eight

~

FOR A MOMENT, I didn't know what to do. Storming out of the house dramatically is more effective if you have somewhere to storm to. Feeling in the pockets of my coat, I found my wallet but not my car keys. I'd left those on the kitchen counter. So I walked. I couldn't go to my folks' place because my mom would ask hundreds of questions about what had gone wrong between Tina and me. I didn't want to lie to my mom, and I certainly couldn't tell her the truth. I was approaching the town center when I saw the entrance to a hotel. It was a tall, square, nondescript building in gray concrete. For want of anything better to do, I walked into the empty lobby. Seeing no one at reception, I rang the bell. A door behind the desk opened and a girl walked in.

Even in my bewildered state, I was struck by her gothic appearance. Her face reminded me of Chrissie Hynde at about age twenty-five. She had jet-black hair and eyebrows. Her pale-blue eyes contrasted with black eyeliner and thickly mascaraed lashes. Her full lips were shiny with coral-pink gloss. Worryingly thin, she was under five feet tall. She wore a dark-blue jacket over a white blouse with a matching blue scarf tied loosely around her neck. The black badge above her left breast read "Charlotte," along with the name of the hotel. Her face relaxed naturally into a sad, soulful look. But when she saw me, she smiled, showing two rows of perfectly white teeth. 'May I help you?' she asked. Her voice was high-pitched but croaky, like she'd had too much to drink and smoke the night before.

'A room, please.'

Her small, chalk-white fingers moved quickly over the computer keyboard on the desk. 'Single or double?'

'Single,' I said, my voice catching. I'd checked in to a single room the week before. But that was for work, and I'd known I'd be going back to Tina in a couple of days. This time, it seemed unbearably sad to be checking in to a hotel alone. I wondered if I should go home, but I could imagine Adam's knowing smirk as he turned to Tina and muttered, 'I told you he'd be back.'

'I need a few details,' said Charlotte. When I told her I lived in the same town, she looked straight at me with those large pale eyes and bit her lip. She took a key from a hook behind the desk and handed it to me. 'You're on the fourth floor. You won't be disturbed there.'

I didn't tell her I wanted to be disturbed. I would have loved it if Tina had burst in saying, 'Rob, come home: I can't live without you.'

I took the elevator up to my room. It was bigger than I expected, with a deep, soft carpet, and a large double bed in the center. I needed to pee, so I went into the en-suite and slumped down on the toilet. It was a good-sized bathroom with a shower big enough for two. If Tina had been there, we'd have showered together before falling into bed. As I peed, I looked down. I did still have a pair of balls; I'd just forgotten how to use them. There were still some spots of toothpaste on them, but it didn't hurt anymore, so I didn't bother washing them off.

I came out of the bathroom, wondering what to do next. The

bed was taunting me. *Look how big I am—just for you, all by yourself.* I turned on the television and hopped between thirty different channels, but I couldn't concentrate. Everything that had happened kept coming back into my head. I had an image of myself, naked, apart from a shirt over my head with toothpaste on my balls. I didn't want to believe that this ridiculous figure was me. And Tina's words had been terrifying. 'I need to experience the darkness.' I didn't want to think about where that would lead her. I had to quiet my mind, and I'd seen the door to the bar next to the reception desk. I picked up my phone and went downstairs.

The bar was quiet, with just three tables occupied. Not wanting anything that reminded me of Tina, I ordered whiskey—a drink she'd never liked. I sat at a table by the window. The view of the office block across the street held limited interest, so I looked at my phone. Tina hadn't tried to get in touch. My screensaver was a picture of her on top of the Arc de Triomphe in Paris with the lights of the Champs-Élysées behind her. She was gazing at me with so much love that I found it impossible to look at her. How had things become so badly screwed up between us? Obviously I knew the answer to that question, but I didn't want to face it. I needed to change the screensaver. Looking through the photos on my phone, I saw several of Boris. For the first time that day, a tear rolled down my cheek. I hadn't thought about him. It's something all men should remember: before you storm out of the house, stop to collect your dog. Tina and Adam would look after him so he'd be okay, but he'd also miss me terribly. I couldn't look at the photos anymore so I put my phone away and drank the whiskey straight down. Unfortunately, it *did* remind me of Tina. She and I had drunk whiskey after Mark had rejected her the night of Emma's wedding. *In those days, she still needed me*, I thought. I went back to the bar. I couldn't think of any drink that wouldn't remind me of Tina in some way, so I said, 'Another one, please. Make it a double.'

The barman had obviously been trained in the art of up-selling. 'Maybe you'd like to buy the bottle, sir. It might work out cheaper.'

If I drank a bottle of whiskey, I'd be in a coma for the next two days. But just then, that sounded like a good plan. 'Okay, put it on my bill.' I had no idea how much it cost, and I didn't care.

I felt conspicuous walking back to my table but I sat down and poured myself a glass. I looked at my phone again. There was still no message from Tina. 'Is that all for you?' asked a distinctive voice. Charlotte, the girl from reception, was standing beside me. She'd taken off her uniform jacket and was wearing a sleeveless white t-shirt. On her right arm was a tattoo in black and dark green that showed a cross encircled by a thick plant stem with some vicious looking thorns. She'd also removed the scarf to reveal a pretty blue and purple butterfly tattooed on her neck below her left ear.

'You can have some if you want,' I said, 'but I don't want to get you into trouble.'

'My shift finished at nine. I can do what I want now.' She sat opposite me. 'Hope you don't mind me joining you. You looked like you needed some company.'

'Yes, I do,' I said. 'I'm Rob.'

'I know; I checked you in.'

'You must check in hundreds of people every day. Do you prefer Charlotte or Charlie or—'

'Charlotte's fine.' She had an empty glass in her hand, so she must have been fairly confident I'd let her join me. I filled it. 'So, Rob, fight with your wife?'

'Not another one!' I said, throwing up my hands.

She frowned. 'Another what?'

'There's this guy I know who can work out what everyone's thinking, from a look or one word. How did you know I'd had a fight with my wife?'

'It happens a couple of times a day. A guy comes in on his

own, and oh look, he lives right here in this little old town.'

'And I thought I was unique,' I said, wistfully.

'We're all much the same,' she said, taking a sip of her drink. 'Did your wife come home and find you in bed with someone else?' With a playful smile, she added, 'Do tell me to fuck off if I ask anything too personal.'

'No, it's fine.' The whiskey was eroding my inhibitions, so I told her something close to the truth to see what she'd do. 'My wife, Tina, was at the dinner table with her stud, Adam, and her friend, Emma. Tina and Emma were both topless. I was on the sidelines with Emma's husband.'

Charlotte's eyes widened. I think it's fair to say she wasn't expecting me to say *that*. 'So, a normal Sunday night?'

I drained my glass, and without stopping to think, told her, 'I'm a cuckold.' It occurred to me that she was the second person I'd told in less than a week. Until now, I'd kept it under wraps. Maybe this was me coming out. Soon I'd be going on cuckold pride marches, chanting, 'We're cucks! Not schmucks! We like to watch our wives get fucked!'

'Interesting,' she said, 'but I'm not sure I approve.'

'You believe in the sanctity of marriage?'

She gave me an *Are you kidding me?* look. 'I don't believe in marriage at all. I'd rather someone stayed with me because they wanted to than because they were contractually obliged.'

'So what's your issue with cuckoldry?'

She leaned forward with her hands in front of her. 'The erotic kick comes from the idea that the woman is doing something wrong. Adultery is a sin and sinful women are sexy. In a world where women were genuinely free to do as they chose, there'd be no cuckolds. You'd just say, "My wife's with someone else, which is her perfect right," and not give it another thought.'

I wasn't sure how to respond to this at first so I took another gulp of whiskey. 'But Tina *is* free to do what she wants. She often says she has the best of both worlds—freedom to enjoy other men and the security of marriage.'

'And what agreements did you put in place?'

'Well, I have to be there.' I thought back to the conversation I'd had with Tina after I arrived home on Wednesday. 'Or, at least, she tells me about it afterwards. That counts as me being involved, apparently.'

Charlotte's mouth twisted into an impish smile. 'So she's free to do whatever she wants—as long as she's turning you on in the process.'

This was uncomfortably close to the complaint Emma had made about Ben.

'Well … I suppose …' I mumbled, looking down at the whiskey in my glass.

Charlotte patted my arm. 'Sorry, Rob. I didn't mean to knock you. I've no right to judge. But if you'd agreed this was going to happen, why did you walk out?'

'The situation got out of hand. Tina forgot that it's supposed to be exciting for both of us, not just her.'

I thought Charlotte might continue along the lines that Tina could do whatever she wanted whether I found it exciting or not, but she just murmured, 'We've all been there.'

We both looked out the window, sadly.

'So what about you?' I asked, turning back to her and refilling our glasses. 'I'm guessing you're not married. Are you seeing anyone?'

'Not at the moment,' she said, slowly. She watched me closely, as if trying to gauge my reactions. I did my best to keep my expression neutral. 'I broke up with Natalie a couple of months ago.'

I was actually relieved. Even after a few whiskeys, I understood that it would be a mistake to do anything. But some harmless flirtation might make me feel more like a normal guy and less like a toothpaste-covered freak. And what could be more harmless than flirting with a girl who wasn't into guys? 'So you're a …' I began, but trailed off, realizing it sounded like a stupid question.

'A what?' she asked with exaggerated innocence.

'Well … you're a ….'

She dropped the innocence and curled her lip ironically. 'You can say the word, you know, Rob.'

'Lesbian?'

I was surprised when she sat up straight and answered with a firm, 'No! There's no such thing.'

'No such thing as lesbians? Millions of porn-watching men are going to be disappointed.'

'Send them my apologies. But if you'd asked Julius Caesar if he was gay or straight, he wouldn't have had a clue what you meant. He fucked whoever he found desirable at the time. And that's the natural thing for people to do.'

I didn't realize I'd changed the way I was sitting, but I must have, because she rolled her eyes and said, 'I see you puffing out your chest and declaring that you're Rob, a hundred percent red-blooded male and all about the pussy.'

'I didn't actually say that, but I think I *am* straight,' I said, trying not to think of touching another man's cock and balls earlier that evening.

She looked skeptical. 'So this guy, Adam … what's his dick like?'

'Well, it's …. I can't say I've noticed.'

She laughed. 'You're not a great liar, are you, sweetie?'

I shook my head resignedly. 'Well, maybe I have noticed. It's a bit bigger than mine. But the interesting thing about it for me was that it was inside my wife.'

'You remind me of those guys who say, "The worst thing about watching porn is trying to ignore the men!" If that were true, wouldn't all guys in porn have *tiny* dicks so there'd be less to block out? When you watch porn, you're checking out the hot women *and* the huge dicks.'

I couldn't be sure she was wrong about that, so I tried to steer the conversation back to her. 'You're bisexual, then?'

She shrugged. 'You can use that word if you want, but it

doesn't help in terms of classification. Since all people are bisexual to some degree, you might as well just say I'm human.'

I remembered Tina saying, 'I even wanted Emma.' I didn't think Tina had ever questioned her sexuality. She'd started dating boys at an early age and never looked back—except in our fantasies. But now I wondered if Charlotte was right. Perhaps Tina was bisexual—or just human.

The whiskey was starting to dull my thought processes, but I ventured, 'So it's society that labels us as …?'

She recoiled, looking appalled by my amateur sociology. 'Don't blame it on society. It's us. We love labels.'

I raised my eyebrows. 'Do we?'

She nodded emphatically. 'When we're young, we spend so much time asking ourselves, "Who am I? What am I?" If we call ourselves gay or straight, at least we know what we are, even if we're not always happy about it.'

I decided it was safer to avoid generalizations and stick to the specifics of this case. I poured her another drink and asked, 'What happened between you and this girl, Natalie?'

It turned out I wasn't any safer here. 'She's not a girl.'

'Sorry. Woman.'

'I'm not even sure there's such a thing as women.'

My head was spinning. 'No women? *All* men are disappointed now—apart from the gay ones.' I caught myself in time. 'Not that there's such a thing as gay, of course, and probably no such thing as men.'

She laughed. I joined in. 'You're learning … slowly. We're all mixtures of male and female. Natalie was a person who presented predominantly female characteristics.'

'So what happened between you and this wom … between you and Natalie?'

'For ease of conversation, we can use the words "woman" and "man," so long as we remember that femininity and masculinity are fluid constructs.'

'I won't forget.'

She downed her drink and took a sip of mine, even though the bottle was on the table. 'How shockable are you?'

I spread my hands in a broad gesture. 'Think back over what I've told you this evening.'

She shook her head. 'That doesn't prove anything. People are strange when it comes to sexual predilections. What *I* like is healthy and life-affirming. What *you* like is sick and should get you locked up.'

'Hey, do what you like so long as you don't hurt anyone else.'

'What if *I'm* the one getting hurt?'

'If that's your thing.'

'I have many *things*,' she said, 'and that's one of them. The motto for my relationship with Natalie was that line from the Lady Gaga song.'

She gave me an enquiring look, and I realized this was a test. I managed to pull something from the depths of my memory. 'It's got to hurt to be fun ... or it's not love ... baby?' I hazarded.

She laughed. 'More or less.' The closest thing Tina and I had to a motto was, "I do not have high hopes for his future." I couldn't help thinking that Charlotte and Natalie's sounded more interesting. 'So you're a masochist ... or do they not exist, either?' I asked.

She nodded as if satisfied with the progress I was making. 'You're definitely learning. Everyone's a masochist and everyone's a sadist. With all these things, each person is somewhere on the spectrum. I lean more toward the masochistic end and I guess you do too.'

My mind went back to the scene in our dining room. Ben was a true masochist and he'd loved it. I'd been turned on by some things, but ultimately I couldn't stand it. 'I'm not sure,' I said.

'Maybe you aren't into spanking or nipple clamps or anything like that. But you like watching your wife with other men. And I bet you get excited when she tells you how much better they are than you.'

'That's my favorite,' I admitted. I had a flash of Charlotte in bed with another man, turning to me and sneering, 'So much better than you.' The thought excited me. I told myself it was just the whiskey and I shook myself out of it.

'You like being humiliated,' she said. 'That's masochistic. And do the other men in Tina's life ever call her a whore and a slut?'

'Yes, but—'

'So you enjoy her humiliation, as well. That's sadistic. Meanwhile, she likes humiliating you and being humiliated herself. So she's both masochistic and sadistic too.' Charlotte had started speaking very quickly so I couldn't say anything. 'The problem I had with Natalie was that she had no concept of limits. She didn't understand that there are different ways of hurting someone. Some of them belong in a sado-masochistic relationship and some of them don't.'

'She broke the rules,' I said, quietly.

I don't think Charlotte heard me, because she carried on, 'At first, it was just physical domination. She used to spank me before sex. That was great: I got into that big time. Then she started slapping my tits and pussy. That was fine too. But it moved on to more psychological domination. I had this little china dragon in my room. She asked me where it came from. I told her it was a present from my first girlfriend, all I had to remember her by, and that I'd had it for years. She threw it against the wall so hard that it didn't break: it shattered.'

I gave Charlotte a sympathetic look. 'She sounds awful.'

'But it was a turn-on.' I thought of all the times Adam had ripped Tina's clothes and understood what Charlotte meant. 'If there was a CD I particularly loved, Natalie would hold a penknife to it and make me beg her not to scratch it. I had to tell her all the things she could do to me if only she'd spare the CD. She always destroyed it anyway.' Her expression was something between a nostalgic smile and a grimace as she recalled, 'And then we had incredible sex. But it moved on to financial domination. It was my job as the more submissive one to pay for everything. Every drink, every meal.' She looked straight at me again, like she was daring me to be shocked. 'Every vibrator. Every whip and pair of handcuffs.'

I just nodded understandingly and said, 'I've never had that, exactly. But Tina likes to make me buy sexy lingerie for her to wear when other guys come round. She said she doesn't mind wasting my money.'

'There's something nasty about that. Even a sub should be allowed financial security.'

I looked at her for a moment. She had come over to a stranger and asked for a drink. She was confidently expressing her views on life. Sitting at the table, she projected a large presence, despite her diminutive frame. 'It's hard to imagine you as a sub,' I said.

'Well, you don't look like a cuckold,' she responded. 'We choose to play a particular role sometimes. We don't always have much choice about how that role plays out. Anyway, when Natalie had smashed all my stuff and cleaned out my bank account, she left.'

'You're better off without her,' I said.

She poured herself another glass. 'Of course I am. But there's one problem.'

I looked into her eyes and understood. 'You're still in love with her.'

She nodded and sniffed sadly. I wanted to put my arms around her, but I didn't think I knew her well enough for that. So I reached across the table, took her hand, and squeezed it. 'It's like you,' she said. 'You're mad at Tina right now, but you're still desperately in love with her.'

'Yes,' I said. There was no point in denying it.

We sat and drank for a while. We were both thinking of someone else. She wiped her eyes with her hand and saw me looking at the thick bush of dark hairs under her arm. 'News flash,' she said. 'Women have hair. Are you horrified?'

'Not at all. It's just not what I'm used to. Tina shaves … everywhere.'

She shook her head in disapproval. 'Because women's bodies need to be refined and processed before they're acceptable. Hairs shaved, plucked, and waxed. Natural scents neutralized with chemicals. Feet forced into crippling high heels to make us the right height.'

I took a moment to feel guilty. Tina had started shaving her legs and armpits long before she met me. It had never occurred to me that she was doing it to make her body "acceptable." It was just part of her routine. She had asked me to shave off her pubes because she thought another man would like it. But I was always telling her how good she looked with a shaven cunt and how much I enjoyed licking it. Maybe I *had* made Tina feel she needed to refine and process her body.

I thought it best to change the subject. 'Can I ask you something, Charlotte? It is personal.'

She laughed. 'We've already gotten quite personal, sweetie! I'm all ears.'

'It's not about sex.'

'Aw,' she said, sticking out her bottom lip in a way that made me want to hug her even more.

'You're obviously smart—'

She rolled her eyes again. 'So why am I working in a hotel? If one more person asks me that ….' She took a sip of her drink and started a story she'd probably told several times before. 'You're right, I've always been smart. That's not bragging: it's the truth. But I didn't get on well at school. I was one of those "she could do so well if only she applied herself" kids. But I *was* applying myself to other things. I wrote books about serial killers. I drew a comic strip starring a cop who was also a vampire. I was throwing so much at the wall, I was sure something would stick and I'd never need qualifications. I managed to focus on schoolwork long enough to get into a third-rate college, but that didn't work out. I spent a lot of time in the library, reading.

But I always found books that were more interesting than anything on the course. I flunked out after a year and took a series of jobs, ending up in this place. And by the way, there are a lot of smart people working here. These days, we can't all get investment-banking jobs. This place isn't too bad. The general manager's an asshole but the front office boss is cool most of the time. I have my own room, I can help myself to anything the guests don't eat, and they pay me enough to buy books and clothes. I also get to meet nice people like you.' I smiled gratefully at the compliment. 'So what's your story?'

I told her about meeting Tina at college and my decision to go into teaching. I made her laugh with some tried and tested anecdotes about students I had known. I even shared with her the details of my cuckold odyssey and told her of Tina's encounters with Steve, Kieran, and Adam. Charlotte managed to hide her disapproval of cuckoldry.

We talked until eleven o'clock and finished the bottle between us. Charlotte had matched me shot for shot, but, despite being much smaller than me, wasn't much affected by the alcohol. I stood up and immediately had to grab the table for support. I sat back down. 'It's because I haven't eaten properly—just a few mouthfuls of chicory salad.'

'Yes, *that's* the problem,' she said, with gentle sarcasm.

'And I don't normally drink this much.'

'No shit. Come on; let's get you up to your room.'

I stood up again. She took my arm and steered me to the elevator. We went up to my room. I sat on the bed while Charlotte took my key and went out. She came back a moment later with a pack of toiletries. 'There are always some of these in the housekeeper's room,' she said. 'At least you can brush your teeth before bed.'

'Thank you,' I said, resisting the urge to flop down on the bed immediately.

'Would you like me to stay with you?' she asked. I don't know what look passed across my face, but she immediately reassured me. 'Don't worry, I'm not going to take advantage of you in your vulnerable state. But I reckon you could use a friend right now.'

'You've already been a great friend,' I said and started crying drunkenly. I couldn't stop myself.

She sat next to me and put her arm around me. 'It beats me why Tina ever needed another man—what with a big, butch guy like you in her corner.'

I stopped crying and laughed instead.

I went into the bathroom, brushed my teeth, and washed my face. When I came back into the bedroom, Charlotte had taken off her trousers. On her right thigh, she had a crudely drawn pentagram tattoo. 'A guy I used to know did that. Not his best work. This one's better.' She turned around to let me see her left calf, which showed a crow sitting on the branch of a tree. It was beautifully rendered in subtle shades of gray and black.

I took off my t-shirt and trousers. She watched me calmly and didn't look either aroused or revolted when I was down to my shorts.

She lay on the bed. 'You can hold me if you want to,' she said, quietly. Lying next to her, I put my arm around her slender midriff, carefully avoiding anywhere too intimate. My last thought as I drifted off to sleep was that she smelled wonderful. I'd assumed from her voice that she smoked, but she hadn't all evening and there was no smell of cigarettes on her. She was wearing a perfume that had strong notes of absinthe. But underneath that, there was sweat. She hadn't neutralized her natural scents with chemicals. My cock automatically straightened out as I breathed them in. I moved my groin away from her so she couldn't feel it.

I either went to sleep or passed out—I couldn't be sure.

Chapter Nine

~

I WOKE UP THE next morning and wondered where I was. Light was coming into the room from a different angle than I was used to. I felt sick and disoriented. My brain was too big for my skull and the whiskey had burnt holes in my empty stomach. But worse than that was the sense of shame and despair as I remembered the night before. I'd allowed things to happen to me that I didn't want. And when I finally stood up for myself, it ended with me walking out on my wife. Why had I asked her to choose between me and Adam? Never go into a conflict unless you're sure you can win.

I also remembered thinking it would be a good plan to get drunk. As I tried to keep my eyes open without throwing up, this no longer seemed such a good idea. I thought about being with Charlotte. That had been the best part of the evening. I'd talked to her and I'd seen hairy armpits and tattoos but I had no images in my head of intimate body parts, so I was fairly sure nothing had happened.

She rolled over sleepily and half opened her eyes. She woke up fully with a start when she saw me. I think she'd forgotten she was sharing a bed with someone. 'Oh, hi,' she said. She relaxed again after she remembered who I was.

'Good morning,' I said, my voice coming out in a thick growl. 'What time is it?'

I looked at my phone. 'Eight twenty.'

She nodded calmly. 'My shift doesn't start until eleven.' She put her head back on the pillow.

'More to the point, what *day* is it?' I asked.

'Monday.'

'Shit, I thought it was Sunday.' I sat up quickly. 'My first lesson starts at nine.'

'Can you make it?'

'Just about, but I've only got the jeans and t-shirt I was wearing yesterday. I don't have time to go home and change.'

She jumped out of bed, looking unaffected by a night of hard drinking. 'You get a quick shower. I'll be back in a minute.' She pulled on her trousers and headed for the door. 'And, Rob,' she said, on her way out, 'there's some mouthwash in the pack I got for you last night. Use the whole bottle if you have to. I'm blitzed just from your breath.'

I showered, brushed my teeth, and gargled half the bottle of mouthwash. I went back into the bedroom, wearing a towel. Charlotte had already returned with a blue shirt, black trousers, and a vivid scarlet tie. 'You can find everything in lost property,' she said. 'I hope they fit.' She handed me a bottle of perfume. 'Your sweat has a barroom tang, as well. Douse yourself with this. Don't worry, you won't smell too girly.' I sprayed it on myself. The strong combination of clove and patchouli masked all other scents.

'I suppose I'd better let you get ready,' she said, with a hint of sadness.

I was in a hurry, but there was one thing I had to ask. 'Charlotte … why?'

She looked at the floor. 'Why what?'

'You hardly know me, but you've treated me like I'm your best friend.'

She shrugged slightly. 'Like I said, you looked like you needed some company.'

'You might have a drink with someone because of that but ... all this?'

She gazed at me with those pale eyes again. 'Some people just smell right.'

The night before, I'd smelled of whiskey, toothpaste, and despair. There was no way that could be right. 'You smell pretty good, too. Thank you for everything.'

'You bought me a drink and let me talk to you. I did okay out of it, as well.'

'Can I give you a hug?'

'Of course you can.'

I put my arms around her slight body. I released her and she went out.

MY HEAD WAS STILL aching as I hurried to work. I didn't want to be moving at all, so elbowing my way through the busy streets was the last thing I should have been doing. I thought about Charlotte. Was it the old cliché of two ships that pass in the night? I'd told her things I hadn't told my oldest friends. We'd spent the night in the same bed and she'd seen me in my shorts. Did that mean anything? I also thought about Tina. She still hadn't tried to contact me. Did she care how or where I was? Did she want me back?

Nobody said anything as I went into the teachers' lounge and poured myself a large coffee. It wasn't unusual for teachers to arrive at work hung over. Fortunately, I had a full day, and being in front of a class of Japanese businessmen made me forget everything else and focus on the job. My last lesson with them finished at five in the evening. I hung around after I'd dismissed the class, hoping someone would come and ask me a question. Anything to delay the inevitable. Nobody did, so when I was alone in the classroom, I took my phone out of my pocket and called Tina.

'Hello, Tina Matthews,' she said in her business voice. I took it as a small good sign that she still called herself Matthews.

'Hi, it's me,' I said, as brightly as possible.

'Hello,' she said again, this time in the same metallic voice I'd heard the night before.

'How are you?'

'Fine.'

There was an awkward pause. I wasn't sure what to say next. 'So … what do you want to do?'

'About what?'

'About the situation. About us.'

'I don't know, Rob,' she said. Even over the phone, I could sense her anger building. 'How did you feel about "the situation" when you flounced out?'

'I couldn't take it anymore.'

'If you were uncomfortable, all you had to do was say, "Guys, this is getting too much for me. Can we take a time out?" But instead, you wrecked something that everyone else was enjoying and totally embarrassed me. Adam would never have done that.'

There were times when being compared to Adam was not at all sexy. And when she put it like that, it did sound like I had behaved badly. 'Well … I'm sorry,' I said.

'Hmm,' she said, as if an apology wasn't enough. 'You think you know better than me what I should do and where my boundaries should be.'

'No, it's just that one of *my* boundaries is that I don't want to be blindfolded and covered with toothpaste.'

'That's your choice. So stand up and leave the room. Don't spoil it for me. And don't try to protect me. *I'm* the only one who can judge what's right for *me*.'

There was another pause. I was about to ask a question and

I didn't know if I could bear to hear the answer. 'Tina, do you want me to come home tonight?'

This time, the pause went on for far too long. 'To be honest with you, Rob, Adam and I are quite happy.'

'You know that from one night?'

'It was a good night. After you left, we called Ben and Emma and got them to turn around and come back.'

I couldn't stop myself from asking, 'And what happened when they came back?'

'You'd know if you'd stuck around, but you didn't, so that's none of your business.'

I tried a joke. 'Will you tell me if I clean the bath again?'

She didn't laugh but her tone softened slightly and there was genuine concern as she asked, 'Are you okay, Rob? Do you have somewhere to stay?'

'Yes.'

Her voice hardened again. 'Then stay there for the moment, please. Goodbye.'

There was a click and the line went dead. A great heaviness descended on me. It was the lowest point to date of my cuckold odyssey. In some ways, it was all too familiar: Tina had decided she was better off with her stud than with me. But at least when Tina had moved out to be with Steve, she'd left me with a home. I'd told her I had somewhere to stay, but how long would that last? I did a quick calculation and worked out I could stay in the hotel for another three days on what I had in my checking account. If I withdrew some of my savings, maybe I could manage two weeks more. Tina had asked me to "stay there for the moment." How long was "the moment?" A week? A month? The rest of my life?

I went to the teachers' lounge and ate a couple of cookies. I wasn't sure if I was going to get anything else that night. I wondered how long a man could live on coffee and cookies.

I walked slowly back to the hotel. I was hoping to find Charlotte behind the reception, but another woman was there instead. I took out my wallet and was about to check in when, on a whim, I asked the woman, 'Is Charlotte around?'

She nodded and opened the door behind the desk. 'Charlotte, there's a gentleman here to see you.'

Charlotte came out of the office and raised an enquiring eyebrow. 'Hi, it's me,' I said, lamely.

'Yes, it is,' she agreed.

'Can I talk to you a minute?'

She came out from behind the desk and we walked into the middle of the reception area where we couldn't be overheard. 'You remember I was telling you about my wife and her lover? Well, she doesn't need me to be the third wheel anymore and I was wondering ...' I trailed off. What exactly was I wondering?

She nodded sympathetically. 'Have you eaten?'

'No.'

'Come on.' She took me through a door marked *Staff Only*. 'If anyone asks, say you're the new general assistant.'

I immediately saw the difference between the staff areas and what the guests saw. The corridor was bare floorboards and the paint was peeling off the walls. Charlotte opened a swing door, and we were hit by a cloud of steam. We went into the kitchen, where it was uncomfortably hot and there was a bad smell of old fat and strong detergent. Eight people were running around, all in white hats, white jackets, and black-and-white-checked trousers. She waited until she caught the eye of a large, black man. He came toward her, grinning. He had red stains on his jacket and his white paper hat was soaked in sweat. 'Hi, Joe,' she said.

'Hey, Charlotte, how's it going?' he asked.

'Still living the dream.'

He laughed like this was the funniest thing he'd heard in a while. 'Living the dream,' he echoed. 'There's no one like you, Charlotte.'

'Some might say that's a good thing, sweetie,' she replied. 'This is Rob; he's the new GA.'

He shook his head at me and chuckled. 'Run, my friend! Run while you still can.'

'So what's not selling tonight?' she asked him.

He looked sad. 'They're not touching my lasagna.'

'They must be insane,' she said. 'I love your lasagna. Could you spare a couple of those for me and my boy?'

'Sure thing,' he said.

While I wondered what being Charlotte's boy would entail, Joe put two brown earthenware dishes onto plates and scattered some salad vegetables around them. '*Bon appétit,*' he said, as he handed the plates to us.

'Thanks, Joe, you're the best,' she said.

'No, *you're* the best,' he replied with another grin.

Holding the plates in front of us, we went out of the kitchen and continued along the corridor until we reached a rickety service elevator. She pressed the button for the eighth floor and we got in. The elevator door opened onto another shabby corridor. The wallpaper looked like it dated from the 1970s. Great flaps of it had come away from the wall. Here and there, it had been stuck back on with masking tape. She took a key out of her pocket and unlocked the last door on the left. 'This is why I try to wangle my way into the guests' rooms whenever possible,' she said, with a wry smile.

It was a basic room, twelve-by-eight feet. A single bed was bolted to the wall opposite the door. There was a closet in pale, cheap-looking wood, and a brown carpet that had worn thin in several places. She had a large pile of books by her bed. Some of them were what I'd imagined—true crime, conspiracy theories, gender studies, popular sociology. But there were also a number of romances. What surprised me more, though, were the posters on the wall—glossy shots of Beyoncé and Mariah Carey. 'You weren't expecting that?' she said.

'I thought you'd be more into Bauhaus and the Sisters of Mercy.'

'It's all about balancing light and shade. I like to have some pop princess chirping away while I'm reading about serial killers and satanic rituals.'

At one end of the room was a converted cupboard into which a toilet, basin, and shower had been crammed. The basin was full of water, and four cans of beer were bobbing around. She fished out two cans, dried them, and handed one to me. We sat on the bed. 'Not the best meal you've ever had,' she said, 'but you won't starve.'

After we'd finished eating, she asked, 'Do you want to stay here tonight?'

I looked around. 'Is there room?'

'The bed's small but so am I. It'll be a squeeze, but we'll manage.'

'But—'

'You're still in love with Tina and I'm still in love with Natalie. We'll be able to control ourselves. All we're going to do tonight is keep each other warm.'

Tears welled up in my eyes. 'Thank you, Charlotte,' I said. 'Thank you so much.'

'Are you going to cry every time I see you?'

'Probably.'

She kissed the top of my head. 'You're a big girl.'

She went into the bathroom and changed into an old red t-shirt. I couldn't do much except strip down to my shorts. I got into bed first. She slotted herself into the space that was left. 'You're going to have to hold on to me to stop me falling out,' she said.

I put my arm around her middle, again taking care not to go anywhere near her breasts. She turned the light out and I lay there, thinking it was strange how life could turn out. I was in a tiny room that smelled of lasagna, holding on to a girl I barely knew, but who had shown me so much kindness that my heart was ready to burst with gratitude.

Chapter Ten

CHARLOTTE ALLOWED ME TO stay the next night and the one after that. Two weeks later, I was still there and we'd gotten into a routine. In the morning, we took the service elevator to the ground floor and she let me out by a back entrance. She told me the kitchen was manic in the morning and Joe didn't work the early shift, so she never bothered with breakfast. I walked to the language school and had coffee and cookies. After I finished work, I went back to the hotel and waited at the back door for Charlotte to collect me. Joe gave us something to eat and we spent the evening in Charlotte's room. Sometimes we watched TV or read, with Beyoncé or Britney in the background.

But often we just sat on her bed and talked. She was interested in philosophy and happy to listen as I told her everything I could remember about ethics, metaphysics, and the theory of knowledge. 'For an English teacher, you know a lot about this stuff,' she said, one evening.

'My dad was a philosophy professor at our local college.'

She nodded slowly. 'That must have been interesting.'

'It was,' I said, scratching my shoulder, 'but confusing for a kid. He knew the arguments for the existence of God, but also the ones for his non-existence. He knew the advantages and disadvantages of both right- and left-wing politics. Nothing was certain. Nothing was absolutely right or wrong.'

She frowned as she thought about this. 'I think I agree with him.'

'So do I, most of the time. But when you're a child, you crave certainty. When I was six years old, my pet rabbit Nibbles died. I asked my dad if rabbits go to heaven. The correct answer was, "Yes, son, of course they do." But instead, I got a forty-five minute lecture on whether our concept of heaven makes any sense.'

I must have looked sad, because she smiled sympathetically and asked, 'So what do you think? Do you reckon you'll be joining Nibbles someday?'

I shook my head. 'I doubt it. He was a good, sweet-natured rabbit. If any rabbits go to heaven, he's up there, having a great time. But I suspect if I come face to face with God, he'll point me to the down elevator.'

She raised her eyebrows. 'You're a nice guy.'

'But I can imagine God saying, "Okay, Matthews, which part of *Thou shalt not commit adultery* did you fail to understand?" '

'*You* haven't committed adultery.'

'He could still get me on several counts of being an accessory,' I said, deciding not to mention Danielle.

In our discussions, I was careful never to disagree with her too strongly. I was painfully aware that there was no reason why she should let me stay with her and that she could tell me to go at any time. So I set out to be as unannoying as possible. I tried to gauge when she wanted to talk and when she wanted to be quiet. I took up as little space in the bed as I could and didn't fart until she was asleep.

It worked. We were living together in a confined space, but we had hardly a cross word. She wasn't one of those people who got along with everyone. She often said she wanted to strangle the general manager and most of the guests. Maybe it was still that I smelled right or perhaps there was something about me that made her feel comfortable. I felt the same about her. We clicked.

Only one time did she look pissed off with me. 'You never talk about your family,' I remarked one evening.

'I don't see my mom and dad.' She folded her arms across her chest. 'They freaked when I introduced them to Natalie.'

'They didn't approve?'

'I'd already told them I was attracted to women, and they seemed fine with it. I didn't think there'd be a problem when I brought Natalie home. It turned out they could handle the *idea* of me with another woman when it was just an abstract concept, but not when it had a face.'

I knew what she meant. The idea of Tina with another man had been a lot easier to cope with before it had a face.

'I had a huge row with my folks,' she continued, looking at the wall, 'and I've never spoken to them since. I send them a Christmas card every year, but I don't put my address on it, so I don't know if they want to reply or not.'

I nodded. 'You don't talk about your friends much, either.'

'No,' she said briefly.

'Are most of your friends back home where your folks live?'

That's when I saw the annoyed look. 'Rob, you remember I said you could tell me to fuck off if I asked anything too personal?'

'Yes.'

Her pale eyes looked straight into mine. 'The same goes for me. Fuck off.'

I never mentioned friends and family again, and after that, we were fine.

I wanted to find a way of paying her back for her hospitality, but it wasn't easy. She refused to take any money. If I invited her out to dinner, she said she'd rather take her chances with Joe. If I suggested going to the movies, she said she had enough

DVDs in her room, and anyway, she'd end up stabbing the people who texted all through the film. Occasionally, she let me take her to a bar. Charlotte drank a lot. I never saw her drunk, but she never went a day without alcohol. We couldn't go to the hotel bar again, in case someone noticed that the new general assistant wasn't doing much work around the place. But there was another bar two blocks down. When we went there, I made sure I paid for *everything*. I also stopped at the supermarket two or three times a week to keep her room supplied with beer.

IT WAS SUNDAY EVENING, three weeks after I'd first met her. My over-thinking mind made me ask, 'Why do you let me stay here?'

'I like having you around,' was her simple reply.

'So what are we?' I asked.

She rubbed her left earlobe between her finger and thumb. 'Is this another of your dad's philosophical questions?'

'I mean, are we friends? Or are we—?'

'You're Rob and I'm Charlotte. Do we have to be anything more than that?'

I knew I should shut up at this point, and for once, I did.

'There's a vending machine on the floor below,' she said. 'I'll get us some snacks. You pick a film.' She handed me a cardboard box full of DVDs and went out. In amongst the titles like *Halloween* and *Friday the 13th* were a number of romantic comedies. When she came back in, I held up *When Harry Met Sally*. 'Really?' I asked.

'It's my favorite piece of erotica,' she said, with a grin. I'd seen the film a couple of times, but I'd never picked up on that aspect of it. 'It's Meg Ryan's ultimate role as the ditzy nice girl. I would *love* to spend a weekend corrupting Sally.'

'I'd like to see *that*,' I said. 'But shall we just watch the film for now?'

She put the disc into the player and we sat on the bed

together, our backs against the headboard. We shared a bag of peanut M&Ms and a bottle of Coke.

After we'd finished the snacks, she raised her arms to stretch. Seeing me looking at her hairy armpits, she shuffled down so that she was lying on the bed. She put both arms behind her head. 'Go on; you know you want to,' she said. I wasn't sure exactly *what* I wanted to do. But I lay down next to her and kissed her armpits, inhaling deeply at the same time. 'Do you like them?' she asked.

'Er ... yes ...' I said. It reminded me of the first time I tried wine after years of drinking lemonade. It was a new and complex flavor. I didn't know if I liked it immediately, but I was fairly sure I'd like it a lot soon.

'People have made money from convincing women that their natural fragrance is vile,' she said. 'But my armpits are pheromone faucets. Put it this way, how's your dick right now?'

'He's taking an interest,' I had to admit.

She smiled knowingly. 'Do you want to go and deal with it?'

'No, I'll be fine.'

We sat up, she put an arm around me, and we watched the rest of the film like two teenagers at the movies.

It was ten o'clock when the film finished, so we went to bed. Charlotte changed in the bedroom, while I was in the bathroom. When we were both in bed, Charlotte turned the light off, but she couldn't get comfortable and kept changing position. Finally, she lay on her back. Even in the dark, I could see the moist twinkle of her open eyes. 'Can't sleep?' I asked her.

'No.'

'What's wrong?'

'I'm horny,' she said through gritted teeth, as if it was the last thing she wanted to be.

'Right ...' I said, in a neutral voice.

'I keep thinking about Natalie.'

'She was a bitch.'

She sighed. 'I know, but I could use a bitch in my bed right now.'

I had plenty of experience of being in bed with a woman who was thinking about someone else. 'Do you …?' I began, tentatively. I remembered the words she'd used earlier. 'Do you want me to go away while you deal with it?'

I felt her lips on mine as she kissed me. I could tell it wasn't a sexual advance: it was more of a bless-your-heart kiss. 'You are such a nice guy, Rob,' she said, affectionately. 'You could have whipped your dick out and said, "I've got a cure for horniness right here, baby!" But you're not like that. It might be because you're still in love with another woman.'

'Or it might be because *you're* still in love with another woman.'

'True … but we are two people in bed together. Maybe we could … help each other.'

'What do you mean?'

'There's something Natalie used to do.'

'You don't want me to steal all your money, do you?'

'Are you joking as a defense mechanism?'

'Yes.'

'Well, stop it. I want you to …' she trailed off. Even in the dark, I could sense an embarrassment that I'd never known in her before. She'd been open about discussing her views on sex, but now, she seemed shy. 'I can trust you, can't I, Rob?'

'Of course you can.'

'Is there … any chance you could spank me?'

I wasn't sure what I'd expected her to ask, but it wasn't that. For a moment, I was too surprised to say anything. My next reaction was to worry about what this would do to my relationship. But this time, my concern wasn't about my relationship with Tina, but with Charlotte. Whatever we had, it seemed to work, and I didn't want anything spoiling it. Could we introduce something like that and then carry on as before? But my cock was very much interested by the idea and came up with a strong counter-argument: *If you reject her, that could also spoil your relationship.*

'I've never spanked anyone before,' was all I could think of to say.

'Teachers sure have changed since the olden days.'

'I think there'd be complaints if I spanked Japanese businessmen,' I said, still joking to cover up my worries.

'I'm sure some of them would enjoy it,' she said. 'Anyway, it's not complicated. You just kind of hit my ass with the flat of your hand.'

'I figured that much out. Do I have to say anything—call you a bad girl?'

'No, you're not doing it because I'm a bad girl. You're doing it because I like it.'

'And how will I know if I'm doing it too hard or not hard enough?'

'I'll say, "You're doing it too hard," or "Not hard enough." Do you think you can follow that?'

'Yes, sorry. Tina says I'm an over-thinker.'

'And it's best if you don't talk about Tina while you're spanking me. That would be odd. You can *think* about her if you want.'

'Okay.'

She'd gone to bed in a long black t-shirt. Her hands were under the quilt and I guessed she was pulling the t-shirt up to her waist. I felt her pushing the quilt away and rolling onto her front. I reached down and my hand found the small of her back. 'Feel around until you get to my ass,' she said. 'It's the one with the crack.'

The first touch of my hand on her butt hit me like an electric shock. It was very small with only the slightest outward curve. Her skin was so soft, I could imagine it bruising if a fly landed on it. My cock was throbbing, and I had to remind myself I was doing this for her pleasure, not mine. I raised my hand and let it fall gently. It was more of a tap than a spank. 'Harder than that,' she said. I put more power into the next one. 'That's it,' she said. 'Don't be afraid, sweetie. Whatever you give me, I've had a hundred times worse.' I spanked her hard six more times. I wish the light had been on so I could see her cheeks turning red. But her throaty groans of pleasure were so arousing that I was finding it hard to keep my breathing under control.

'There's something else Natalie used to do,' she said. If I wasn't allowed to talk about Tina, I didn't think Charlotte should be talking about Natalie, but I let it go. 'She used to select an area for what she called "serious pain." She used to smack it, scratch it, and smack it some more. It hurt like crazy but made me purr like a kitten. I want you to try it.'

I chose the upper part of her right buttock. As accurately as I could in the dark, I spanked the same place four times. My nails were short, but I pushed them into her delicate skin and dragged them across the sore area. 'Okay, now, Rob, go for it! Hard as you can.' I lifted my hand up high and brought it crashing down on her. The sound was so loud, I was sure it echoed round the whole building. I did that three more times. 'Now give me the scratching of my life. Get some blood if you can.'

I dug my nails into her as deeply as possible and raked them across her buttock. I smacked her again twice more, putting all my strength into it. I stopped and waited for her reaction.

'That was good,' she said. It was nice to get a positive review. 'For your first time,' she added, ruining it a bit. 'Okay, Rob, fair's fair. You've done something that turns me on. I should do your favorite now.'

I was already massively turned on, but I wasn't going to refuse. But what did she consider to be my favorite? Was she going to pick up another guy in the hotel bar and fuck him in front of me?

'You like being teased about your wife's other guys being better than you, don't you?'

'Oh yes,' I said, my cock quivering in anticipation.

'Okay, try this. You love Tina's tits. They're big and soft. You love to touch them and squeeze them. You want to cover them with kisses. But you're not the one doing that tonight, are you?' I thought I'd been excited while I was spanking Charlotte, but now my heart pounded and my cock tried to force its way through my shorts. 'Adam's the one who's touching her tits tonight. And she loves it. She goes wild for his touch, doesn't she?'

'Yes,' I said, my voice hoarse with excitement.

'He's sucking her nipples and doing everything you should be doing right now. But she prefers it when *he* does it. When *he* touches her, she turns to jelly. When *he* fucks her, she feels like a real woman. She's finally getting the fucking she desires and deserves. Why does she love his dick so much, Rob?'

'Because it's better than mine.'

'Repeat after me: *Adam fucks! Rob sucks!*'

I was breathing so heavily, it was difficult to say anything. 'Adam fucks! Rob … oh no!'

'Oh, sweetie, are you okay? Have you had an accident?'

'No, I thought I had, but I managed to stop it. I will if you say another word.'

'Okay, go into the bathroom and do what you have to do,' she said. 'I'll stay here. I'll call you when I'm finished, but I've got a feeling it won't take long.'

It didn't take either of us long and soon, we were back in bed.

'Thank you,' I said, kissing her shoulder.

'It's still Tina who turns you on,' she said.

That wasn't the whole truth anymore. At that moment, I thought Charlotte was one of the sexiest women I'd ever met. And I loved the way she'd gone from cruel teasing to compassion in an instant. I went to sleep more confused than ever.

Chapter Eleven

~

THE NEXT MORNING, THE alarm went off at eight o'clock. Charlotte took some clothes out of her closet and went into the bathroom, closing the door behind her. I dozed a little but was woken by a scream. It wasn't a scream of horror, just surprise. I thought maybe she'd seen a spider. A few minutes later, she came out, dressed for work. She stood in front of the bed and turned her back to me. Pulling down her trousers and panties a few inches, she showed me the top part of her right butt cheek. There were four livid scratch marks surrounded by black bruises.

My mouth fell open. 'I am so sorry!' I said.

She pulled her trousers back up, came over to me and kissed my forehead. 'Don't be,' she said. 'You did exactly what I wanted you to do and I enjoyed every second of it.'

I didn't feel as guilty as I thought I would, despite having broken the rules. While Charlotte and I hadn't had sex, I couldn't deny we'd had a sexual experience. However, I wasn't sure I still needed to play by the rules. I didn't know if I was still in the game. My main worry was that Charlotte would spend the day thinking about the night before, decide it was a mistake, and throw me out.

I had the opportunity to find out how things were going at home. I desperately needed a change of clothes. The trouble with relying on lost property was that most of the guests who forgot things weren't my size. Every evening, I washed my socks, shorts, and shirt in Charlotte's sink, then dried them over her radiator. She liked to keep her room tropically hot, so they were always dry by the morning. But people at work had noticed that I wore the same clothes every day. I don't think they were convinced by my comments about, 'all those blue shirts I've taken to wearing recently.'

I sent Tina a text and asked if she could bring me some clothes. I also hoped … well, what did I hope? Did I want her to beg me to come home? I wasn't sure anymore. I remembered telling Ben that I could never go back to a life without cuckoldry. Now, I didn't know if I wanted to return to the emotional roller coaster of life with my wife and her lover. I enjoyed staying with Charlotte. It was quiet and routine—with just one interlude of intense excitement so far. And I couldn't say to her, 'Thanks for putting a roof over my head, but I don't need it anymore so I'll be seeing you.'

Tina texted me back, saying she'd meet me after work at a coffee shop in the center of town. At lunchtime, I bought a pack of disposal razors and shaved as best I could in the teachers' bathroom. I wasn't sure what I wanted from the meeting, but I wanted Tina to find me attractive.

I WALKED INTO THE coffee shop, trying to look positive and confident. Scanning the room, I saw a familiar face, and my shoulders sagged. It wasn't Tina. It was Adam. He waved at me and held up the suitcase that Tina and I normally took on vacation. I went over to his table and sat opposite him.

'Hello, Rob, it's good to see you,' he said, with a broad smile.

'Mm,' I said, in a non-committal voice.

'Tina sends her apologies. At the last minute, David asked her to dial in to a teleconference.'

So send anyone else in the world, but not Adam!

He handed me the suitcase. 'Here are some changes of clothes.'

'Thanks. How's Tina?'

'Very busy at work, so she's stressed, but I think she's enjoying the new challenges.'

It struck me that this was the sort of thing a husband says when asked about his wife. *I* should have been the one talking like that about Tina.

'Is Boris okay?'

He nodded reassuringly. 'He's fine. He misses you, though.'

I noticed he didn't say my wife missed me—just my dog.

'And how are you?' It was only polite to ask.

'Not too bad. Ben and Emma come round often.' He looked at me keenly to see how I'd react to this.

'So, you and Emma …?' I asked in a resigned voice.

'We've had some fun,' he said, and there was that self-satisfied grin again. Not content with fucking my wife, he was also fucking the object of my sad little crush.

I knew it would be more dignified to say nothing, but I had to ask, 'How does it work … with you, Tina, and Emma?'

'It works well,' he said, with more than a little triumph in his voice.

The masochistic side of me wanted him to give me all the details. I wanted him to be the alpha male, bragging about what he'd done to my wife and my friend. Did he make both of them get on all fours on the bed with their asses pointed at him? He could spend some time fucking Tina from behind, and when he got bored, pull out and thrust into Emma instead. Or perhaps he made them fight over him. The first to score three falls or a submission won twenty minutes of Adam love. Either way, he was a lucky bastard. But, I reflected, did *he* get to spank Charlotte?

'You might want to come back to the present, Rob,' he said, clicking his fingers. 'Where are you staying?'

'I've … stumbled on a good deal at a hotel,' I said.

'This good deal,' he said, with a knowing smile, 'what's her name?'

I should have realized he'd work that out. 'What gave it away?' I asked, with a weary gesture.

'You smell of strawberry and vanilla shower gel. The stuff you find in hotel bathrooms is more generic. And it's not what a guy on his own would buy for himself.'

Why couldn't Charlotte have chosen a more gothic shower gel? 'I have a friend,' I admitted, 'but nothing's going on between us.'

He probably knew that wasn't exactly true, but he spread his hands. 'I'm in no position to judge.'

'You most certainly are not,' I agreed, with anger creeping into my voice. I took a deep breath and tried to calm down. 'Look, Adam, I don't know if you and I are friends exactly ….'

'I've always liked you, Rob.'

'There are things I like about you, and things I don't. But can I ask you one thing? Can you *please* not tell Tina anything about this?'

'I am the silent tomb,' he said, placing his hand on his heart.

'Thank you,' I replied, but wasn't sure if I could trust him. After all, he had told Emma about Mark being with Tina on Emma's wedding night. He must have known that was confidential.

'Why don't you come home?' he said, in a voice that was almost entreating. 'Bring your friend, if you want.'

'What, so you can fuck all three of them?' I exploded. There was a family sitting at the next table. They turned to look at me. 'Sorry for the language,' I muttered. They went back to their pancakes and ice cream.

'That wasn't what I was thinking,' he said.

'So, what were you thinking?' I asked, more quietly. 'Surely it's the perfect setup. You have sex with two beautiful women and no one's there to get in the way.'

'Ask yourself something, Rob,' he said, speaking as if he were giving an explanation to a not very bright student. 'You met me in a cuckold club. Why do you think I was there?'

I shrugged. 'Most single men go there to pick up married women for sex.'

'And I could have done that if I'd wanted to.'

It must be nice to have that level of confidence.

'But I came up to you and Tina, because I wanted to get to know *both* of you. I didn't want to fuck a married woman. I wanted to fuck a *happily* married woman.'

I ran my hand over my face. 'You wanted to fuck her in front of the man who loves her.'

'Exactly,' he said, nodding.

'And then you waited until Tina was in love with you before you fucked her friend in front of her?'

He looked impressed that I'd worked that out. 'Yes, I did.'

I sighed. 'I know why you do this. I keep saying that a cuckold relationship is about love. But you are messing around with very strong emotions here. Someone's going to get hurt.'

'If Tina gets hurt, I'm sure she'd like to have her husband around. And Emma wouldn't mind having a sympathetic friend to talk to.'

I looked at the table for a while. I wanted to see Tina again. I could imagine Boris leaping for joy when I came home. I was excited by the idea of Emma being part of our cuckolding scenario, but …. 'If I come back, will I end up with a shirt on my head and toothpaste on my balls again?'

He gave me a sympathetic look. 'That got to you, didn't it? I'm sorry. I should have realized and stopped things before they went so far.'

'It's not your responsibility to look after me. And it wasn't just that. The whole situation at home was getting to be too much for me.'

'Maybe if I back off … give you and Tina more time to yourselves.'

Would that be possible? Could Tina and I go back to spending our evenings watching crime dramas with our dog stretched across our laps? It was a nice thought.

But then I remembered the unflinching certainty in Tina's eyes after I said, 'It's him or me.'

I shook my head. 'She's made her bed; now you can all lie in it together.'

He nodded. 'I understand.' I had the feeling that he *did* understand, and for a moment, I felt something close to affection for him. Then he asked me a question I hadn't been expecting. 'Would you like to see Emma naked?'

I raised my eyebrows. 'You've got pictures?'

He laughed. 'No, but there's an event this Saturday you might be interested in. You remember Emma posed for *Society Women*?'

'Of course I remember. Has her issue come out yet?'

'Not yet. Her pictures are only available online.'

'What's the address?'

'It's a deep-web forum for members only. But once a year, Spencer organizes a show. He's asked Emma, along with the other *Society Women* models, to take part. Tickets are expensive, going for several hundred on eBay. But I can get you a couple of freebies.'

'What sort of show will it be?'

'It's different every year, but I promise you, there'll be some surprises.'

I was intrigued. 'All right.'

He opened his wallet and took out a wad of tickets. He slid two across the table. 'There you are. Why don't you bring your friend?'

'I don't want Tina meeting her.'

'Tina won't be in the audience. Why would she want to watch a lot of naked women?'

'I'll suggest it to Charlotte.'

'Great. See you on Saturday. It's a dress-to-impress event. Your old suit was looking scruffy, so I bought you a new one. It's in the case.' So now I was getting handouts from my wife's lover.

He stood up, indicating the meeting was over. On the way back to the hotel, I stopped at a newsstand and bought a copy of *Society Women*, which I put away in the suitcase.

As I walked, I found myself appreciating Charlotte even more. Without her, I would have been forced to go back home by now. Adam still wanted me to be part of the games he and Tina were playing. But somewhere along the way, what *I* wanted had been lost. I understood that there was something inherently submissive in the role of cuckold. The archetypal dominant male does not sit and watch while another man fucks his wife. But I was still human and had the right not to be pushed into things I didn't want to do. However much Tina and Adam told me that I just had to say no, their games had a momentum of their own. If I went back, I would get caught up in them again. I couldn't handle that … not yet, anyway.

Charlotte was waiting for me in the usual place at the back door of the hotel. She gave me a welcoming smile, so I guessed she wasn't about to tell me to leave. I hugged her. She was so tiny in my arms, it was like holding a sparrow. She hugged me back, but as we separated, she looked at me, surprised. 'What's that for?'

'For being a friend. For taking me in like a stray puppy.'

She took my hand in hers and squeezed it. 'You're better company than a puppy.'

When we were in her room, she asked me, 'What's in the suitcase?'

'Clothes. I wanted Tina to bring them, but she sent Adam instead.'

'How are things at home?' she asked, casually.

'Fine, as far as I could tell. Adam said I should go back.'

I thought I saw fear flash across Charlotte's face, a look she quickly replaced with indifference. 'Are you going?'

'No, I'm going to stay here for now,' I said, and added quickly, 'if that's okay with you, of course.'

She sighed—I guessed with relief—then shrugged. 'It's up to you.'

I put the case down on the bed. 'Adam bought me something.' I opened the case and took out a well-cut black suit, a tuxedo, and a black bow tie.

'That's nice,' she said. 'Try it on.'

I took off my clothes and put on the suit. 'You look great, sweetie!' she said.

There was only a face mirror in her bathroom, so I couldn't see myself full-length. But I had to admit my shoulders and the top of my chest looked good. 'I don't know if I can accept it,' I said.

'Someone bought you a present. Don't be ungrateful. But … why? Is evening wear compulsory for teachers these days?'

I wasn't sure how to pitch this to her. 'Are you free on Saturday night?'

'Yes. I finish at five on Saturday. After that, I'm off until Monday.'

'Would you like to go to … an event?'

'What sort of event?'

'I don't know exactly.' I paused. I wasn't sure how she'd react when she found out it was an event organized by *Society Women*. 'Have you ever seen this before?' I asked, taking my copy of the magazine out of the case and handing it to her.

She looked through it, her face revealing nothing, and gave it back to me. 'Bland and inoffensive,' she said. 'Some of the women are hot.'

'One of Adam's friends runs it. Once a year, he puts on a show. You might get to see these hot women looking bored live on stage.' I could see her wavering. 'And if the show's no good, we can have a few beers and pass judgment on the people in the audience.'

That settled it for her. 'Okay, I'm in.'

Chapter Twelve

~

O**N THE NIGHT OF** the show, I put on my new suit, tuxedo, and bow tie. I still thought I looked smart, but I paled beside Charlotte. It was the first time I'd seen her dressed for a night out. She looked stunning in a floor-length dress. The corset was black and tied at the back with crisscrossed ribbons. It was sleeveless, so her thorny cross and hairy armpits were on display. The skirt consisted of multiple layers of scarlet and black lace. Around her neck she wore a Sid Vicious style chain and padlock. Her hair was hanging loose over her bare shoulders. 'You're fantastic,' I said, kissing the top of her head as she applied the finishing touch by painting her nails black.

'I don't want to get lost in amongst all the beautiful women.'

'No danger of that.'

We took a taxi to the address printed on the tickets. As we walked in, I wondered if Tina would be there. Adam had said she wouldn't, but I already knew he couldn't always be trusted. He might be interested to find out what would happen when Tina met Charlotte. Me with another woman …. Would Tina see that as a gross violation of the rules? A loud voice in my head said, *Fuck the rules!* Tina thought she could enjoy herself and explore all those "dark places" that fascinated her so much, and she probably assumed I'd be there to pick her up afterwards if she wanted me to. It would do her good to see me with another woman, especially one who looked as striking as Charlotte did that evening. We were playing a new game now—one where I made my own rules.

We were in an old theater that looked like it had been hastily renovated for the evening. The floor was bare wood with rows of bolt holes where the original seats had been. The auditorium was laid out in cabaret style. There were about sixty round tables with eight chairs at each one. The chairs faced a wide proscenium stage with red velvet drapes that had once been elegant but were now old and dusty. Running across the back wall of the auditorium was a temporary bar constructed from glass blocks illuminated by purple LEDs. Twelve barmaids, each in a waistcoat and bow tie, were opening champagne bottles and mixing cocktails. Spencer had obviously sunk a lot of money into this event. But if he'd been aiming for shabby chic, he hadn't managed it. The old style stage didn't match the garish modern bar. It was difficult to heat a room this size so people were jiggling their legs and hugging themselves to keep warm.

Adam waved to us. Spencer was sitting next to him, but Tina was nowhere to be seen. Despite my bravado of a moment ago, I was relieved: it would be a less stressful evening without a face-off between Tina and Charlotte. Adam pointed to someone who needed our company. Ben was at a table on his own. He looked suave in a made-to-measure tuxedo and had a bottle of champagne on the table in front of him, but he looked uncomfortable—like a man who knew his wife was about to appear naked in front of a roomful of strangers.

'Good evening, Ben,' I said, 'may we join you?' He gave me a look of such pathetic gratitude that I wanted to hug him. He hastily pulled out two chairs from under the table. 'This is my friend, Charlotte. Charlotte, this is Ben.'

I'm sure Ben hadn't been expecting me to arrive with a woman, particularly one like Charlotte. But he endeavored to make polite conversation with her, while I looked at the other people in the audience. At some of the tables were groups of young men. They were well-dressed, swilling down champagne and teasing each other in loud, braying voices. They were the only people who seemed to be genuinely enjoying themselves. The older men were equally well-dressed, but looked impatient for the show to start. There were very few women in the audience.

When he ran out of things to say to Charlotte, Ben held out his hand to me. 'Sorry that things got … well, I'm just sorry.'

I shook his hand. 'Don't worry, buddy. None of this is your fault.'

I'd assumed Spencer would host the show, but he stayed in his seat as the lights went down. Onto the stage came a ginger-haired guy in his twenties who was wearing a white shirt with a red bow tie and jacket that clashed horribly with his hair.

'Good evening, ladies and gentlemen,' he announced, his voice becoming distorted as he spoke too loudly into the microphone. 'It's been a busy day, preparing for tonight's show. I've spent all afternoon with the girls, helping them undress. It's a good thing I'm gay and have no interest in naked women.' He sniggered and looked round the room. 'Well, that's what I told them, anyway.' He paused and waited for a laugh that never came. I felt sorry for him: he probably had dreams of being a stand-up comedian and thought a gig like this was a step on the right path. But Spencer had said no one was here for the music and they weren't here for the comedy, either.

He carried on gamely, 'There's a girl tonight you're going to love. I call her Noisy Neighbor because she keeps me up all night.' With still no reaction from the audience, he started to sweat. 'There's another one I call Hot Water Bottle. She makes me hot, but if I'm not careful, she makes my bed wet.' The only reaction was exasperated groans. I thought it only a matter of time before the young men threw empty champagne bottles at him. He gazed imploringly in the direction of the wings and must have gotten the signal he wanted because he turned back to the audience, looking relieved. 'And now, the moment you've all been waiting for. Ladies and gentlemen, please welcome the *Society Women* women.'

I thought he could have put that better, but it was the first thing he said that went down well with the crowd. Everyone applauded, and there were some cheers and whistles. He made a relieved exit and the stage lights went off.

The stage was dark for a minute. Someone in the wings started playing "Fever" on a muted saxophone. A single spotlight picked out the downstage-right area. A woman stepped into the light. She was naked apart from a white mask that covered the whole of her face. I couldn't understand why she was wearing this. An ornate Venetian Colombina over her eyes might have been elegant, but this mask was just strange. It wasn't scary like something out of *Halloween* or *Friday the 13th*. (I'd learnt something from my time with Charlotte.) It was just blank and featureless. She walked slowly across the stage. Reaching the center, she turned to show the audience her butt. Despite the light being on her, she shivered. I felt uncomfortable, watching her. But the rest of the crowd approved. The older men clapped while the younger ones nudged each other and pointed. A second naked woman followed her onto the stage. She also had a great body—slim and toned with beautiful breasts. But she wore the same blank mask, which made any expression impossible. Three more women trooped onto the stage, all wearing the same masks, all doing the same turn when they reached the center. People were clapping, cheering, and hammering on the tables. As the sixth masked woman stepped into the spotlight, Ben leaned his head toward mine. 'That's Emma,' he whispered.

And there they were. I did what Tina vowed I would never do and saw Emma's breasts. I could cross that one off my bucket list. They were lovely—small, perfectly round, with cute pink nipples. They sat up high on her chest without even a hint of sag. But although she was nude, I'd never seen her looking less sexy. She had a beautiful, expressive face. Why would anyone ever think it should be covered up?

My problem with the masks was that they drained the women of all character. Then I realized: *that is the point.* The people in the audience didn't want these women to have personalities. They were marks of success. *I can afford a big house, a fast car, and women with fantastic bodies like these.*

Charlotte watched, stony-faced. She didn't like what was happening any more than I did. I looked at her. She wasn't as conventionally attractive as the women on the stage. People might have said she was too short and thin and that her tits and ass didn't have the right sensual curve. But her face, hair, armpits, clothes, and tattoos all screamed out her individuality. Something moved inside me, and I realized I loved her. I put my arm around her and gave her a squeeze. She kissed my cheek quickly and turned her attention back to the show. There were nine women on the stage now—standing in a row, not moving, letting the men appraise their bodies.

A tenth woman stepped out from behind the drape, and I immediately sat up. She was wearing the same mask as the others, but I had no trouble recognizing her. I had spent more than seventeen years worshipping those breasts and burying my face between those legs.

I felt the same snapping inside me as when I was in the dining room with toothpaste on my balls. Tina was not a beautiful body to be put on display. Whatever had happened between us, she was still my wife, still my best friend.

I stood up and strode toward the stage. Charlotte scrambled to her feet and was soon right behind me. I didn't know if she understood what I was doing or if she just supported any attempt to break up this show. Spencer made a move to get up, but Adam put a restraining hand on his arm. As I climbed onto the stage, I realized Ben was also with me. No one tried to stop us. The people in the audience looked at us curiously; they hadn't expected the show to take this turn, but they were interested to see what would happen next. I went straight to Tina. I took off my suit jacket and wrapped it around her. This attracted a few boos from the crowd. Ben did the same thing to Emma. Neither of them offered any resistance as we hurried them into the backstage area.

As we stepped into the wings, the ginger-haired host looked at us blankly and shrugged. He plainly didn't care anymore what happened to the show. The saxophonist raised his eyebrows, but kept on playing.

Charlotte took the lead. Working in a hotel had given her an instinct for finding her way through the areas where the customers never went. We headed along some dark corridors until we saw a green exit sign. A man was sitting by the door, reading a newspaper. He stood up as we approached and said, 'Here, you can't—'

'Listen, sweetie,' said Charlotte, 'all five of us are walking through this door right now. Have you got a problem with that?' She was only half his size, but her expression said clearly that she would do appalling damage to his body if he tried to stop us.

He looked into Charlotte's glaring blue eyes and said, 'I guess that'll be okay.'

He opened the door and we found ourselves in the staff parking lot. A path led out to the highway. 'My car's parked down here,' said Ben. 'You guys take care.'

He took Emma off down the road, leaving the three of us standing on the sidewalk. It would have been nice if he'd offered us a ride, but I guessed there was only one person in the world he was thinking about at that moment. I had a protective arm around my own wife, who was shivering. My jacket didn't offer much protection against the night air.

Charlotte hitched up the skirt of her dress and ran out into the middle of the road. Looking the way she did, it was no surprise that she was soon noticed. A taxi stopped in front of her. Opening the back door, she waved us in. I bundled Tina into the car. Charlotte joined us on the backseat and gave the name of the hotel to the driver.

Tina ripped off the mask and I saw her face for the first time that evening. The last time I'd stepped in to save her from an erotic scenario, she'd been furious with me. This time, she put her face against my chest and sobbed. 'Thank you, Rob,' she said. 'Thank you so much.'

I held her in my arms and asked, 'What on earth were you doing up there?'

'Adam wanted me to do it,' she said, when she managed to catch her breath.

No one knew better than I that saying no to Adam wasn't easy, but I said, 'You need to tell him to fuck off.'

I could feel her nodding vigorously. 'I will,' she said. I wondered if she meant it.

We couldn't go through the hotel reception with a naked woman, so Charlotte took us round the back to the staff entrance. We went quickly along the corridor to the service elevator and were soon in her room. I was glad she liked to keep her room so hot. Tina stopped shivering immediately.

I sat on Charlotte's bed and held Tina in my arms. Tina raised her head and looked at Charlotte with a frown. 'I'm not sure who you are, but thank you.' So Adam had kept his word on that at least.

Charlotte sat next to us and put her arms around Tina, as well. When Tina had needed help, Charlotte had stepped up with no hesitation. And now here she was, comforting a woman she'd never met before. I felt a surge of love for Charlotte. But my feelings were complicated by being with Tina again. My love for Tina had had seventeen years to deepen and mature. My feelings for Charlotte were newer, a lot more raw, but real nevertheless. I had to ask myself a familiar question: *What do we do now?*

Charlotte kissed Tina on the lips. I hadn't expected this. Neither had Tina, but all she did was whisper, 'So soft.'

Charlotte gazed at Tina intently, like she was trying to read Tina's mind. Then she untied the ribbons of her corset and let it fall into her lap. The first time I saw Charlotte's breasts was when she showed them to my wife. They were tiny, with no roundness to them—just a slight swelling like two mosquito bites. She had large, reddish-brown nipples, her right one pierced with a horizontal barbell.

I couldn't understand why Charlotte was doing this. The timing seemed inappropriate. Though still dazed, Tina *did* seem to understand what Charlotte was doing. Tina took off the jacket and sat there, naked. Charlotte ran her hand down Tina's cheek, moving onto her neck and shoulder. Tina responded to the tiny hands on her skin, leaning in to Charlotte's touch like a kitten leans in to a stroke.

Tina's breasts appeared huge next to Charlotte's. Charlotte looked at them with a gentle, appreciative smile. 'You are beautiful,' said Charlotte.

'So are you,' said Tina, shyly. 'Is it okay if I …?'

Charlotte put her hands on the bed behind her and pushed her chest toward Tina. 'Help yourself, sweetie,' she said.

Tina bit her lip. It reminded me of the time we'd gone to the zoo and she'd had the chance to touch a boa constrictor— the same mixture of fear and fascination was in her face. She stroked Charlotte's left breast. 'It feels nice,' she murmured.

Charlotte put her hands behind her head and showed Tina her armpits. Tina's eyes widened. She hadn't expected that. 'Kiss them,' said Charlotte. Tina leaned forward and kissed each armpit in turn. 'Do you like them?'

Tina nodded. 'You don't smell like a man.'

'Is my scent turning you off?'

Tina shook her head. Charlotte kissed Tina's neck. Tina

closed her eyes and enjoyed the sensations. I slid off the bed and crouched down on the floor. Charlotte laid Tina down and kissed from her neck down to her belly. It was different than watching Tina being kissed by a man. I wasn't jealous of Charlotte in any way; she wasn't taking my place so much as playing a part I could never play. She kissed the shaven mound above Tina's cunt and looked up. 'Do you want me to …?'

After everything that had happened, Tina seemed to be finding it hard to think clearly. 'I've only been licked by … men before,' she said, hesitantly.

Charlotte gave her a wicked look on a par with Tina's own. 'I can do it better.'

Tina let out a moan and parted her legs. 'Yes, I want you to.'

Charlotte gently pressed Tina's labia together and used them to massage Tina's clit. At the same time, Charlotte easily slid two fingers inside my wife and moved them in and out. Tina made a high-pitched humming noise that turned into a sustained 'Ah!' at the back of her throat. Charlotte moved her hand away from Tina's clit and lowered her head toward it. Charlotte used the tip of her tongue to lick around Tina's labia. Every time she seemed about to cover Tina's clit with the flat of her tongue, she moved it away at the last moment. Eventually, the noise Tina was making formed itself into a word, repeated over and over. 'Please! Please! Please!'

Charlotte lifted her head and asked, 'Please what?'

'*Please* lick my clit! *Please* make me cum!'

Charlotte grinned triumphantly and placed her lips around Tina's clit. I can only imagine Charlotte's tongue was working furiously because it was less than ten seconds before Tina's moans reached an inaudible pitch. She grabbed two handfuls of the sheet under her, lifted her hips, and came with a scream.

Afterwards, Charlotte sat up and wiped her lips demurely. The astonishment on Tina's face seemed to say that everything she'd always believed had been proved wrong. Then she broke into a grin. 'That's it,' she said. 'I'm cured. I'll never look at another man again.'

I hoped she didn't mean that. I think Charlotte was mainly reassuring me when she said, 'Yes, you will.' Charlotte turned to me and said, 'You see, Rob, we're all somewhere on the spectrum.'

Tina looked confused at this, so I explained, 'Charlotte has a theory that we're all straight and we're all gay—to different degrees.'

Tina nodded and gazed into Charlotte's eyes. 'Do you mind if I test that theory?' she asked.

'Do as many tests as you want,' said Charlotte, enthusiastically. As she stretched herself out, she looked at Tina, then at me. 'A married couple in my bed. This is a first for me.'

I could see Tina was nervous as she knelt between Charlotte's open legs. 'Well, *this* is a first for me.'

'I thought you, Adam, and Emma had been all over each other for the last few weeks,' I said.

'It's been more Adam all over Emma and me,' said Tina. 'I've kissed Emma and I've sucked her tits.' *That* was an image I wanted keep in my mind. 'But I've never licked her pussy.'

'You'll be fine, sweetie,' said Charlotte. 'Do unto me as you would like others to do unto you.'

Tina kissed Charlotte's cunt tentatively. She opened it up with her thumbs and licked her clit, moved down to lick her hole, then licked her clit again. She tried licking around Charlotte's outer lips, then around her inner lips. The way she jumped from one spot to another, it was as if she wasn't sure where to go.

Tina stopped, raised her head, and looked at me. 'I don't know what I'm doing,' she said, annoyed with herself. 'With a cock, you put it in your mouth and move up and down. A pussy seems more complicated.'

'Would you like me to show you?' I asked.

'Yes,' said Tina, and did an awkward sidestep with her knees to sit on the bed with her back to the wall. I took her place between Charlotte's legs. I was lowering my head when I realized with a start that Tina wasn't the one who needed to give her consent. Whose cunt was it anyway?

'Is this okay?' I asked Charlotte.

'Go right ahead with your coaching,' she replied. 'The world needs more people who know how to eat pussy. I'm happy to be the demonstration doll.'

'What you were doing was fine,' I told Tina, slipping into teacher mode. 'It's good to kiss and lick different parts of the pussy at first.'

I knew I was supposed to be doing this for Tina's benefit, but even so, I took a second to appreciate what was happening. I was going to lick Charlotte's cunt for the first time. That was a moment that deserved to be cherished. And it was a beautiful cunt. I doubt if Charlotte had ever shaved or even trimmed her pubes. The bush of dark hair was full and thick, just like those under her arms. I gently parted the hairs and found her clit, pink and shiny in the keyhole of her labia. I ran my tongue around the inside of her lips. She tasted so good. I didn't want to admit it, but I thought her cunt was even more delicious than Tina's. I got my mind back on the coaching. 'It's important to listen,' I told Tina. 'If her breathing gets quicker or deeper, you're doing the right thing. If she moans or says anything like "Yes!" keep doing what you're doing. If she's obviously enjoying it, you don't have to mix it up.'

Charlotte didn't seem to mind me talking about her in the third person. She giggled at what I was saying in between moaning as I kissed and licked her cunt. 'Yes!' she said, as I gently but firmly applied my tongue to her clit.

'Now you try,' I said to Tina and moved out of the way.

Charlotte groaned with frustration but laughed at the same time. 'What did you say a second ago, Rob? If she says "Yes!" keep on doing what you're doing! Practice what you preach.'

But she stopped complaining when Tina's tongue touched

her clit. 'Oh yes!' she said, louder and more passionately than before.

'Hold your position,' I said. 'Steady speed. Maintain the same pressure.'

'Listen to your teacher,' gasped Charlotte.

Tina kept licking until Charlotte clutched Tina's hair and pushed Tina's mouth even harder onto her cunt. Charlotte came with a shout of 'Oh, fuck!' that was so loud, I worried other staff members would come running to see what was wrong.

Charlotte took a moment to lie limply on the bed. It looked like all the life had been licked out of her. Finally, she sat up and kissed Tina. 'You did great, sweetie,' she told her. Then she kissed me and said, 'You achieved your learning objectives for that lesson.'

I kissed Tina. The taste of Charlotte's cunt on Tina's mouth was powerfully erotic. I pushed my tongue into Tina's mouth to taste as much as possible.

I thought Tina would be wired after everything that had happened, but her eyes were closing. Events seemed to have exhausted her rather than put her on edge. Even so, she looked at Charlotte and said, 'Just one thing … who are you?'

'I'm Charlotte. Pleased to meet you.' She held out her hand. It struck me that people normally shook hands *before* performing oral sex on each other, but we were making our own rules.

'And you and Rob …?' Tina faltered.

'Are me and Rob, yes,' said Charlotte.

Tina nodded as if that explained everything. She went off to the bathroom and closed the door. I looked at Charlotte. 'Why did you do that?'

Charlotte shrugged. 'Our eyes met and we both knew what was going to happen. Sometimes when you've been through emotional turmoil, you need to release some tension. That's the best way I know.' She paused for a moment and looked at me sadly. 'I suppose if you and Tina are back together ….'

'It looks more like *you* and Tina are together.'

'You know what I mean.'

Not sure what to say, I gave her a hug. I didn't want to make any promises unless I was sure I could keep them. I managed a vague, 'We'll find a way of making it work for everyone.' Charlotte nodded, as if that would do for now.

'We should get some sleep,' said Charlotte, when Tina came back into the bedroom. I looked at the bed doubtfully. 'It'll be fine. We just need to snuggle close.'

Tina lay in the middle of the bed. Charlotte slotted herself in beside her. I squeezed myself in next to the wall and put my arm around both of them. Charlotte was about to turn the light off when I had a thought. 'Tina, is Boris in the house on his own?'

'No,' she said, only half-awake. 'Adam warned me I might not get home tonight, so I took Boris round to Louise's place.'

That was a relief. I could sleep easy now.

Except I couldn't. After Charlotte had turned the light off, she and Tina were soon purring peacefully. But I lay awake. It was partly excitement. No one had felt the need to make *me* cum, so I was still hugely turned on. But in a way, I was glad of this. It meant I could enjoy being in bed with two sexy women. They felt good under my arm and the cocktail of feminine scents was intoxicating. I was also still pumped after rescuing my wife in front of a surprised audience. A man in a tuxedo leaps into action and saves the day. Who did that remind me of? And I would never forget my first experience of watching Tina with another woman. I'd been worried about Tina meeting Charlotte for the first time, but it had gone quite well.

There was something else, though. A number of questions were going through my mind. Why had Adam warned Tina she might not get home tonight? Did they normally have a *Society Women* sleepover after the show? He'd arranged for Tina to be part of the event. He'd invited me. He'd stopped Spencer from intervening when I rushed onto the stage.

I regretted being jammed up against the wall as I maneuvered my way down to the foot of the bed. I managed to get out without waking them and I felt on the floor for my suit trousers. My phone was in the pocket. I went into the bathroom and shut the door so I wouldn't disturb them.

Sitting on the toilet, I texted: *Did you plan this?*

I waited. A moment later, my phone beeped. In the quiet room, it sounded like an alarm going off.

I read the message: *You and Tina belong together. You both needed something to make you realize that. Goodbye.*

I switched my phone off and opened the bathroom door. Tina's eyes glinted in the dark: she'd been woken by the beep. 'Who's texting you at this time?' she slurred.

'Just someone we used to know,' I said.

She was too tired to question me further. I got back into bed and put my arm around both of them again. Soon, all three of us were asleep.

Rob Matthews was born in London. He divides his time between Britain and the United States. He lives with his wife Tina and their dog Boris. Coming soon: a book about interracial cuckoldry, set in England, as well as the next instalment of A Cuckold Odyssey.

Follow Rob on Facebook and Twitter:

www.facebook.com/robertpatrickmatthews

@robandtina1

From Fanny Press and Rob Matthews

~

Tʜᴀɴᴋ ʏᴏᴜ ꜰᴏʀ ʀᴇᴀᴅɪɴɢ *We Make Our Own Rules*. We are so grateful for you, our readers. If you enjoyed this book, here are some steps you can take that could help contribute to its success and the success of this series.

- Post a review on Amazon, BN.com, and/or GoodReads.
- Spread the word on social media, especially Facebook, Twitter, and Pinterest.
- Like the www.facebook.com/robertpatrickmatthews and www.facebook.com/fannypressbooks.
- Follow Rob (@robandtina1) and Fanny Press
- (@fannypress) on Twitter.
- Ask for this book at your local library or request it on their online portal.

Good books and authors from small presses are often overlooked. Your comments and reviews can make an enormous difference.

A Cuckold Odyssey
Books 1 and 2

Come Home With Us

A Cuckold Odyssey

Married couple Rob and Tina enjoy sharing fantasies in bed together, and their favorite involves Tina with another man. One day Tina proposes that they take the logical next step, and they invite her co-worker Steve to their home. Much to Rob's dismay, Steve soon forms his own ideas of how this scenario will play out. A cuckold Rob may be, but he's no pushover.

In their search for new ways to explore the cuckold lifestyle, Rob and Tina meet Ben and Emma. Rob and Tina are happy to offer advice on cuckoldry, but when Tina and Emma start pursuing the same stud, Tina has to face the possibility that she's not the hottest wife in town anymore. And what will be the impact of Adam, an eerily perceptive older man encountered at a cuckold club?

I Can Do It Better

A Cuckold Odyssey

www.ingramcontent.com/pod-product-compliance
Lightning Source LLC
Chambersburg PA
CBHW010449100726
47904CB00008B/2541

* 9 7 8 1 6 0 3 8 1 4 7 8 2 *